NORTH TO ABILENE

To Audrey
with Love from
Her Big Bruvver

NORTH TO ABILENE

CLIFFORD H. FRY

A Black Horse Western

ROBERT HALE · LONDON

ISBN 0 7090 5938 8

Robert Hale Limited
Clerkenwell House
Clerkenwell Green
London EC1R 0HT

Photoset in North Wales by
Derek Doyle & Associates, Mold, Clwyd.
Printed and bound in Great Britain by
WBC Book Manufacturers Limited,
Bridgend, Mid-Glamorgan.

ONE

The two men rode slowly through the heat of the afternoon. The dust being raised by the thirty or so cattle hung in the still dry air like a cloud, and the small herd of mustangs cutting backwards and forwards behind the cattle only added to the discomfort.

Jeff Mason, the younger of the two, was slouched in his saddle, a bandanna covering the lower half of his face, protecting his nose and mouth from the millions of dust motes in the air. His stetson was pulled well down, shielding his eyes from the glare of the sun. The heavy, full-length duster seemed at odds with the heat of the day but the fullness of it gave considerable protecton from the direct burn of the sun. It also kept the glinting particles of sand from the business-like twin Colts strapped about his waist, and in the cold of the night it offered yet more protection.

A quick peek under the tilted J.B. showed a clear young face made to look mean by a badly healed bullet scar on his forehead; the eyes, too, at present a soft blue-grey, could swiftly change to the bleak look of slate on a rainy day.

The man riding beside him had seen it happen, and not too long ago either.

Captain Luke Malloy was no stranger to sudden

death; he'd ridden through the war until its end before rejoining the Texas Rangers, but even Luke had to admit that the young man riding beside him was so goddamned quick with a gun that lightning was slow by comparison. He was also the most goldarnest argumentative galoot he'd ever tried to talk into being a Texas Ranger. True, the young man had eventually accepted the badge, but whether he'd ever do anything about using the damned thing was something else again.

Luke glanced up. Jeff was eyeing him quizzically from under his J.B. the eyes soft with a hint of latent humour.

'Somethin' funny?' Luke grunted.

'Yep,' replied Jeff, wiping his mouth with the tail of the bandanna to get rid of the grit.

'What's funny?'

'You are.'

'How come?'

'You was just about to start out on that ranger bit agin'. Right?'

'What makes you think so?'

'Luke old buddy, you're about as subtle as a hound-dog chasin' a bitch on heat, an' about twice as persistent.'

'Sarah Kyle's got a lot to answer for, teachin' you all these high-falutin words. Afore you know it you'll be too high an' mighty to be a Texas Ranger anyway.'

Jeff fished in his pocket and held up the badge. The gold star on a silver circle glinted in the sunshine. 'See? I've got it with me an' I'll use it if I ever have to. OK?' Jeff pointed to the two burlap sacks tied to the saddle horn of Luke's mount. 'You just keep your eye on that money an' git it back to Casa Verde where it belongs; I'll probably see you again somewhere up around this place they call Abilene in about six months time ... if this trail drive goes according to plan.'

They were approaching a large camp-site where a massive herd of cattle was milling around, while sweating, cursing cowboys were sorting and separating them into bunches according to their brands. The noise was increasing rapidly as they approachd so Luke raised a hand in silent goodbye as he wheeled away on his long journey to Casa Verde.

Jeff replied in kind as he drove his small herd towards the main bunch.

Nodding to the two men who took over the steers he cut out his string of mustangs and roped them in line with the rest of the remuda before striding over to the man who appeared to be in charge of the mayhem that was the beginning of the trail drive to Abilene.

The smell of smoke was in the air mingling with the nose-tingling odour of burnt hair and slightly scorched flesh as cherry-red branding irons seared their markings into the mavericks' hides.

Another young longhorn was thrown to the ground by a sweating cowboy as the man who seemed to be in charge stepped forward with a branding iron held ready.

With expert ease he pressed home the brand, then quickly dabbed a small iron beside the new brand before releasing the animal.

The maverick scrambled to its feet crow-hopping away, bawling its indignation to the world as the big raw-boned man stepped away from it and pushed the irons back into the fire.

Jeff noted that the newly branded animal carried the Lazy Bar K, the brand of Nathaniel Kyle. Jeff was a full partner with Nathaniel, a man he had befriended over two years earlier. The smaller mark beside the new brand looked like two arrow-heads, one behind the other; a road brand which indicated that although there were different brands within the herd, all the animals wearing that particular road brand were under the care of one man: Matthew Tyler.

The big man part-turned as the animal was released and looked over his shoulder.

Jeff guessed the man to be in his fifties but there was nothing soft about him, from his thick heavy fingers and large hands to his balding gingerbread head, this man was as tough as hickory and about as unbending too.

The ice-blue eyes held a question long before the gravelly voice asked, 'You frum Kyle's?'

'Yep,' replied Jeff. 'Mason's the handle,' he continued, as he offered a hand.

'Matt Tyler,' responded the man as he took Jeff's hand in a meaty paw, a big friendly grin spreading across his face. 'Expect to be called mister on the drive. That sit OK with you?'

'Suits me, Mister Tyler,' Jeff answered.

'Good tuh have you along, son, heard you've bin on a drive before, it'll come in handy. Powder River wasn't it?'

'Yep, Bozeman trail. How many cattle you takin'?'

'Did you bring in that other thirty head?'

'Sure did,' responded Jeff. 'Passed 'em over to two of your boys over yonder.'

'Good; that'll make it three thousand head, just about right,' grinned the big man.

'Hear you're gonna turn fifteen thousand dollars worth of beef on the hoof into seventy-five thousand

American, Mister Tyler. Good trick if you can pull it off.'

'Nothin' to it,' replied Tyler with a wry grin. 'All we gotta do is to git em to Abilene.'

'That's all, huh? Over halfway across Texas then through Indian country all the way to Kansas. That's where this Abilene place is I'm told.'

'Jesse Chisholm's done it a few times an' all we have to do is follow his trail,' grunted Tyler.

'Understand Jesse's a half-breed Indian trader; d'you think that might have somethin' to do with him gettin' through the Indian Territories without trouble?' asked Jeff, a note of scepticism in his voice.

'You here to grumble or work?' retorted Tyler. 'Grumblers we don't need, but if you're gonna work it's about time you got started.'

Jeff touched the brim of his stetson politely. 'You're the boss.'

'Good of you to remember. Get your bronc an' start sortin' with the others, we'll finish this conversation along about sundown. Meantime, there's more'n enough to keep us all working – with our hands, if you get my drift,' grunted Tyler, turning back to the fire as another heifer was thrown and held ready for branding.

Jeff stared at the big man's back for a few moments. Tyler was evidently a man on a short fuse, but who could blame him? He had a big responsibility to all the owners and if anything went wrong Tyler would be the man they'd blame. Jeff knew he'd been wrong to question the boss of the drive within minutes of arriving: it could get him disliked by everyone. Nobody wanted a moaner around.

'Guess I spoke out of turn, Mister Tyler. You have my apology, sir.'

Tyler looked up, the big grin back in place. 'So let's see you cutting out the herd, son, huh? No hard feelin's.'

Jeff grinned in return, flipped a finger to his stetson and left to get his mount; he was soon in the saddle of his best cutting horse joining with the rest of the men sorting cattle and mavericks.

TWO

There were only four men including himself sorting the cattle and leading them to the fire for branding.

Conversation was almost non-existent, partly because of the incessant bawling of the herd. The amount of dust the steers disturbed meant that the men had to wear their bandannas over their noses and mouths so talking was restricted to terse instructions, or muttered curses if an animal proved particularly fractious.

Jeff soon realized that there were three different brands: Nathaniel's Lazy Bar K which was a K sitting on a bar; the Circle C-connected which was a small C in the centre of a circle connected by a straight line; and the third brand which was the Lazy P, the P was tilted backwards as if it was about to fall upon its back.

Mavericks were stamped with the same brand as the mother and all animals received the double arrow road brand.

As the day wore on four more cowboys turned up at the camp. One was in his mid-sixties but as fit as a flea. Ward Killick was acting as the cook, and Jeff later learned that he was also representing the Circle C-connected while the Lazy P was represented by a cheerful looking cowpoke of around thirty. Sam Pinter looked a real lady-killer with his light-blue eyes and tight curly hair, but in spite of his devil-may-care attitude Jeff could see that he certainly knew his job as his mustang twisted this way and that, guided only by the pressure of the man's knees as it cut out an animal from the main herd. Then the reata, held loosely in Pinter's hands, would shake out with seemingly effortless ease trapping the selected steer.

The man helping him with the chore was a typical tight-lipped waddy who had been hired on by the trail boss for the duration of the drive. There was nothing to distinguish him from a thousand others ... except that he wore a very businesslike pair of Remingtons set on a cross draw and Jeff guessed Virgil Calder knew how to find them in a hurry. He also carried a Bowie knife fixed to the back of his shell belt and another sticking out of the top of his right boot.

The one man who stopped Jeff in his tracks was Wesley Calvin. The man had ridden up behind him and dismounted as Jeff was taking a well-earned breather. The first indication Jeff had that anyone was near him was hearing a voice with a deep southern accent asking, 'Could y'all direct me to the boss-man, mista?'

Jeff turned ... and stared at the first black cowboy he had ever seen. The man was not overly tall by Texan standards but he was built with the lean muscular grace of a cougar. He wore a faded blue kepi on a head of tight curls sprinkled with touches of frost. The worn Union Army uniform fitted him so tightly that it threatened to burst its seams as the muscular body moved beneath it, and the lighter marks on the arms where the chevrons had been removed, told of previous sergeant status. Jeff instinctively noticed the holster on the man's left hip carrying a Colt Navy revolver, but his eyes were drawn back to the broad ebony face that was split in a wide friendly smile of sparkling white teeth, the smile slowly dying and the sloe-black eyes starting to harden.

'Is y'all hard of hearin' or are you so god-damn' ignorant that you cain't even answer a simple question, mista?'

The tone said the man was used to being obeyed and Jeff realized that he was staring like a dumb foal facing a rattlesnake.

'S-say, mister, I sure am sorry,' he mumbled, embarrassed. 'I ain't usually that stupid, nor ignorant neither. It's just that....'

'You ain't never seen a black feller afore, huh?' the black cowboy interrupted. The big grin was back again. 'Sho' now it ain't the first time it's happened man, an' I done guess it won't be the last.' He stuck out a huge black hand. 'Name's Wesley Calvin, ex-sergeant of the Ninth.'

Jeff allowed his hand to almost disappear in the big man's paw. He was expecting a bone-crushing grip but was surprised at how gentle and cool Wesley's hand was.

'Name's Mason,' he replied, as he pulled the bandanna from his face. 'Mostly called Jeff. I'm real pleased to meet you. The man you want is right over there doing the branding.'

'Wa-al now thank you, mista,' replied Wesley, as he turned to leave.

'Jeff sounds about right,' Mason called after the retreating figure.

Wesley turned and grinned, showing the set of teeth a second time. He touched his kepi in a small salute. 'Jeff it is then. Look to see y'all at supper, man.'

Jeff's eyes followed the retreating figure. Either Wes was insensitive to other people's feelings or he was doing it out of bravado, he ruminated, but it took a lot of courage, or stupidity, to wear a Union Army uniform on a trail drive out of Texas. To his way of thinking it wasn't just asking for trouble, more like going down on his knees and begging for it.

Jeff shrugged aside his morose thoughts, remounted and rode off to continue cutting out the mavericks.

It was some time later, when the sun was dipping towards the horizon that the trail boss gave the signal to start turning the cattle.

The men eased to the outer edge of the herd and began to slowly turn the steers in upon themselves creating a close milling circle. They were much less likely to stampede or turn tail while packed together.

As the darkness closed in three new men rode out from the camp and began to circle the herd while the rest of the men drifted away towards the dark blob of the chuck wagon. They passed their mounts over to the wrangler – a cowboy in his late teens – before removing the saddles and making for the cheery warmth of the camp-fire. Dumping their saddles they formed a line in front of the chuck wagon for their hard-earned meal.

Jeff saw that Wesley Calvin was the first in line; he also realized trouble was looming as a big tough-looking *hombre* dressed in worn Confederate grey stepped in front of the black man.

Wesley tapped the man on the shoulder. 'The end of the line is back there, brother,' he said quietly.

Quincy McBride stared at Wes. 'I don't go second tuh the likes of you-all, *boy*,' he sneered in a deep southern drawl. 'Now git to the back of the line afore I kick yore ass. An' I ain't yore brother. Now, move it!'

Wesley seemed to sigh as his shoulders sagged. 'Guess this God-awful war didn't teach anybody a damned thing, did it? Looks like you an' me'll have to settle this once an' for all, huh?'

'You betcha,' snarled McBride. 'But not with guns, sonny, with *these*.' He held up his clenched fists. 'Time I'm finished, you'll run all the way back up north where you belong.'

'Ain't nobody gonna do nothin',' interrupted the trail boss sharply. 'With that kind of noise the herd would be scattered to Hell an' gone in no time at all. Any differences you two have kin be settled in the mornin'; now git your grub an' eat.'

'I'm staying where I'm at,' growled McBride, his attitude defying further argument.

'You-all kin stay right there fer now,' agreed Wesley evenly. 'We'll settle this in the morning ... *brother!*'

There was none of the usual banter around the camp-fire that evening. Wesley Calvin and Quincy McBride eyed each other silently across the fire, when one moved the other watched him in expectant silence, each waiting for the other to start something.

Both men knew it wouldn't take much to trigger a stampede, but everyone knew it would only take the slightest spark to put the two men at each other's throats and to hell with the cattle.

As the night riders came off watch others were detailed in turn by the trail boss to ride herd on the restless beeves throughout the night.

Sun-up brought an easing of the tension as the cattle spread out to graze and the men once again stood in line for their breakfast.

Quincy McBride was waiting long before breakfast was being served. He was obviously determined to cause trouble for Wes, whose prodigious appetite caused him to be next in line.

McBride had a sneering grin pasted on his face as he waited until Ward Killick opened the serving flap.

The elderly cook stared at McBride for a few moments, then he deliberately placed a large meat cleaver on the board. 'I git any trouble from you or anybody else' – his hand flashed to the cleaver and it crashed into the board almost as quickly as a man could draw a pistol – 'I'll split his skull. Understood?'

There was an uneasy shuffling of feet and muttering, nobody in his right mind ever upset the cook on a trail drive. If anything he was as much in command as the trail boss himself.

Killick paused to allow the men to think about it, then he yanked the cleaver out of the board and pointed it at McBride. 'Yesterday you was first, today you're second. Come on now, move along or I'll throw it to the buzzards.'

Once again the tension began to build as the men ate their breakfast in silence, they all knew that once the meal was over the two men would settle their differences with their fists and it had to be said that McBride was clear favourite to win.

'Ain't anybody gonna have a bet on it?' asked Billy-Joe, one of the young drag riders, his voice pitched high with excitement.

'Who's gonna be stupid enough to bet against Quincy?' asked Sam Pinter derisively.

'I will! Who's gambling?' Virgil Calder was holding a wad of paper money. 'I say the black feller's gonna win. Any takers?'

There was a rush to take Calder's money before it ran out.

'How about you, Mason,' asked Calder, 'd'you want

some of my money too?'

Jeff shook his head. 'Seems to me you might know somethin' I don't,' he grinned. ' 'Sides I'm one cautious feller, my money stays in my poke.'

'Hell, I wished I had some *dinero*,' squealed young Tom Buckley, Billy-Joe's friend. 'I'd sure enough put my dollars on Mister McBride an' no mistake.'

The betting caused further excitement and the men congregated on a clear patch of ground away from the camp and formed a crude circle, while the two combatants walked slowly towards it glaring at each other like a couple of prairie dogs over a bone.

Both men removed their shell belts and passed them to one of the men helping to form the circle before walking slowly into the centre.

Quincy was by far the bigger of the two men but there was hardly an ounce of surplus fat on either as they stripped off their shirts and vests. Their kepis were thrown on the top of the discarded clothing where they lay like an omen from the recent past: one a faded dirty blue, the other an equally dirty grey. The war was over but nothing had changed.

The two men moved around each other vying for advantage, but while Quincy's hands were spread in the groping attitude of a wrestler, Wes adopted a boxer's stance, his hands moving easily as muscles rippled under the ebony skin.

Quincy feinted a snatch hoping to draw Wes into his reach. The black man's left snapped out twice in quick succession, the hard blows smacking into Quincy's face with a meaty thump. Quincy's arms dropped a little in surprise and Wes slammed in a right cross to the face closely followed by a left hook under the heart. Quincy grunted but grinned as he inched closer. Two more punches cracked into his face but he continued to advance, that smile still pasted on his lips.

Wes tried a round-house left to the jaw putting all his strength behind it. Quincy grabbed the fist in mid-flight with his own left hand while allowing his right to slide up under the arm, he locked the right hand behind Wesley's neck and threw him high into the air sending him crashing into the ring of cowboys with contemptuous ease, flooring Billy-Joe and his young friend in the process.

Wes tried to scramble to his feet but Quincy was on him like a tiger, grabbing one arm and twisting it high into Wesley's back before throwing him a good fourteen feet into the other side of the ring of men.

Wes landed on his back with his arm twisted underneath him, it forced a grunt of pain from between clenched lips, then Quincy crashed on top of him, heavy boots gouging into his exposed stomach. The grunt of pain turned into a shout of agony as the boots thumped home.

The men were shouting encouragement and praise as Quincy climbed to his feet expecting the fight to be over but Wes rolled on to his side and slammed his undamaged fist into Quincy's crotch, then both men rolled over and over, clinging to each other, punching, biting, kicking and gouging until they forced each other into a standing position.

Quincy saw his opportunity. His hands moved with expert ease as he turned his opponent so that the man's back was towards him. His thick meaty arms slid inside Wesley's and the hands locked behind the black man's neck.

A deathly silence settled over the watching cowboys; they all knew that Quincy intended to snap his opponent's neck. It would only take a second and every man was waiting with unconsciously bated breath for the ominous crack that would signify the end.

'Enough!' The voice cracked into the silence like a whiplash. The sound of a gun being cocked was loud in the stillness that followed the shout and all eyes turned to Matt Tyler, standing within the circle with a cocked pistol in his hand.

In the hesitation that followed his stentorian shout he stepped up to the two men and pushed the gun into Quincy's neck.

'I said, enough!' Tyler snarled. 'Let him go or I'll blow your damned head off.'

Quincy was holding Wes as if he were a child, the crippling grip rendering the black man powerless. 'He's mine,' panted McBride. 'I beat him an' I'll kill 'im.'

'*I said* let him go!' hissed Tyler. 'I need every man I've got to get this herd through an' nobody's gonna foul it up.' He raised his voice again. 'You heard me, everybody back to work ... *Now!*'

Slowly the disgruntled men drifted towards the remuda and Quincy allowed Wes, now almost unconscious, to slip to the floor, then he too snatched up his clothes and followed the rest.

Tyler slowly turned a full circle to make sure everyone was leaving. He stopped when he saw Jeff Mason still there. 'I said *everybody*, mister.'

Jeff nodded towards the man on the floor. 'He needs some attention otherwise he won't be working for a week.'

Tyler nodded reluctantly. 'You an' the cookie see to it, but once he's on his feet I wanna see you back in there with the herd, OK?'

'You're the boss,' agreed Mason.

'Bet your life I am,' retorted Tyler, as he followed the men. 'An' nobody had better forget it.'

Ward Killick arrived carrying a pail of water and some rags as Jeff knelt to examine Wes.

'Kinda took a beating, huh?' grunted Killick as he too knelt beside the injured man. 'Still, coulda bin worse.'

'How much worse could it get?' asked Jeff as he gently massaged the man's neck.

'Like dead, that's how much,' groused the cook as he slopped water over Wesley's face. 'What did he expect comin' here in *that* uniform?'

He continued to slop more and more water over the man until he opened his eyes.

'Y'all gonna try to drown me now, friend?' Wes asked with a lopsided grin.

'Huh,' snorted Killick as he climbed to his feet. 'You don't *have* to be grateful, fella, but you ain't makin' many friends thisaway.'

He tipped the remainder of the water over the black man's head and marched off.

Jeff grinned at the sight of Wes spluttering under the deluge. 'Never get at odds with the cook,' he admonished. 'You fit to get back to work?'

Wes grunted with pain as he managed, with Jeff's help, to climb to his feet. 'Just about,' he muttered. ' 'Cept I feel as if I've bin run over by a stampede.' He limped over and collected his clothes. 'Next time I have a run-in with that fella I'll use better judgement.'

'Like what?'

'Like this,' he muttered, as he strapped on his gunbelt and patted the gun. 'Ain't nobody gonna treat me thataway twice. Give me a boost into the saddle, friend; a few hours' ridin' herd will soon get the kinks out.'

Jeff eased Wes into the saddle amid many groans and curses until he was comfortable, before climbing astride his own mount and following him towards the herd for another day of roping and branding.

The differences between the two were not over, just buried beneath the surface and threatening to burst into violence as one hectic day rolled into the next until all the branding had been completed.

By this time the cowboys had split into two groups, depending on whether they favoured Quincy McBride or Wesley Calvin.

Mason, Calder and Sam Pinter showed a leaning towards Wes, while Quincy McBride seemed to find favour with a pair of dour, bearded brothers; also southerners judging by their accent. Carl and Bart Simes had been hired on by the trail boss as had McBride so it was perhaps natural that they should link up with him. The two boys considered McBride their hero while the wrangler, Seth Calhoun, seemed to drift between the two factions.

The trail boss tucked his gloves into his belt as he approached the men who were waiting to know their drive positions.

His voice was uncompromising. 'Here's how it's gonna be men. Mason, you ride point with Calvin. McBride and Carl ride swing behind Mason. Bart an' Calder take flank. Pinter, you look after the two drag men, an' Calhoun, take turn about with either of the Simes brothers as relief.'

At the end of the short speech he started to turn away.

'I ain't eatin' their dust,' snarled McBride. 'I'm a point rider.'

Matt Tyler paused, turning only his head. 'You'll do as I say or pack your gear, mister.' The two men stared at each other for a few moments. 'Put up or shut up,' growled Tyler. 'I ain't got all day.'

McBride's eyes slid to Jeff. 'You got any objections to me ridin' point, mister?'

'Nope,' replied Jeff evenly. 'But I figger that if Mister Tyler says I ride point, that's just where I'll be.' Jeff looked at Tyler, the question in his eyes.

'You heard me, McBride,' growled Tyler. 'You either ride swing, swap with Pinter on drag or ride out. Get to it, men, let's move out.'

Tyler swung into the saddle without waiting for a reply and loped off following the wheel ruts left by the cook's heavy wagon as the men mounted and reined towards their allotted positions.

McBride pulled his mount across Jeff's path. 'This ain't over, mister,' he growled.

'Didn't even get started,' replied Jeff evenly.

'Git uppity with me, sonny, an' I'll give you what I gave your pal, understand?'

'No you won't because you won't git the chance, mister.'

'You're that good, huh?'

'Try me or get out of my way, fella.'

With cool deliberation Jeff eased off his right-hand riding glove and flexed his fingers before dropping the hand to his gun belt. 'When you're ready just reach for it.' Jeff's voice still held that soft even tone but his eyes told a different story.

'Not a fist fight then?'

Jeff slowly shook his head.

As if his horse was walking on eggs, McBride gently eased his mount out of the way, the momentary flicker of fear in his eyes saying that he knew how close to death he had come.

'You ride swing until the boss says different,

comprende!' It was not a question but a flat uncompromising statement.

McBride nodded before dragging his horse around and heading towards the herd.

Jeff stared morosely at the retreating figure, he knew that this was no way to start a trail drive. Everyone would, of necessity, be in close contact over the next four or five months, yet there was already a big rift in a body of men who needed to depend upon eath other if they were going to meet the natural hazards of the trail, not to mention the unnatural ones such as Indians, rustlers and stampedes. All would stretch nerves and patience to breaking point under normal circumstances, but with a man like McBride in their midst it was like adding a live match to a keg of gunpowder and hoping nothing would happen.

Jeff gave a dismissive shrug as he spurred towards the front of the slow-moving herd. A black man who had fought for the North mixed with at least three men from the deep South was not exactly the balm he'd recommend for peace and contentment. A pensive smile flicked across his face at the vagrant thought that if the mixture was a drink it would probably blow a man to bits at the first swallow.

THREE

The men had been on the trail for three weeks; the herd had settled down to a steady pace of some fifteen miles a day and generally the drive was going well, but the discontent within the two groups of cowboys had widened to the extent where Seth Calhoun could no longer mix with both factions. McBride had given him an ultimatum coupled with some gentle persuasion which left the young cowboy with a split lip, a badly bruised eye and some sore spots on his body that forced a groan each time he mounted a bronc.

Jeff watched Calhoun ride slowly towards the camp. The evening was closing in fast and there were flashes of lightning in the distance. The sultry air burnt the throat and the grass was tinder dry.

Sam Pinter lifted a hand in acknowledgement as he passed Calhoun to take over his watch, jogging slowly towards Jeff.

'One of those nights?' asked Sam as he approached.

'Herd's kinds restless,' replied Jeff. 'An' that ain't helping none,' he continued, nodding towards the distant flash of lightning in the sky. 'Hope the boss decides to send out some extra help, just in case.'

Sam grunted something as they passed each other on their way to circle the herd in opposite directions.

Static electricity crackled in the air. It would take next to nothing to set the herd off tonight, Jeff thought, as he crooned softly through a lullaby, soothing the cattle as he slowly made his rounds, a sudden flash of lightning across the horns of the herd, a sharp noise, the flap of the end of a poncho in a vagrant wind, just about anything. And to top it all they were entering Indian Territory.

Jeff knew that this particular section was Comanche country, but as they pushed forward they would have other tribes to contend with. The Mescalero Apache, Kiowas and Cheyenne all had their hunting grounds in this section of the Indian Territories.

Deliberately he kept his eyes hooded from the distant flashes so as not to spoil his night vision and all the time he moved slowly on, crooning softly, nerves screwed down under his calm exterior.

Around midnight another shadow appeared out of the night as Bart Simes took over the watch and Jeff drifted slowly away from the herd towards the darkened camp.

Seth Calhoun was wrapped in his bedroll close to the horses and as Jeff eased quietly up to the tether line, Seth groaned softly as he half raised himself on one arm.

'Still hurtin', huh?' Jeff murmured. 'Don't worry. I'll see to it.'

He barely heard the muffled 'Thanks' as he led his mount to the far end of the line, noting as he passed that the horses were wearing their saddles tonight, just in case of trouble.

Jeff was tying his mustang to the line when he noticed two shadowy figures having a whispered conversation. It was too dark to tell just who they were but as they parted he was almost sure from the outline that one was Quincy McBride.

Some sixth sense made Jeff pause before approaching the banked-down fire where the coffee pot would be simmering. The man he assumed was McBride crossed the camp going over close to the chuck wagon where his faction normally bedded down, but the other had only moved a short distance, where he hunkered against the bowl of a tree. A moment later a match flared behind a cupped hand as the man brought the flame to his quirley.

Jeff thought the man was Virgil Calder but the flare of the match had temporarily blinded him so he could not be sure.

He stumbled in the now Stygian darkness making the horses snort restlessly. By the time he'd calmed them and looked for the man, he had gone.

Jeff made his way to the fire, hunkered down and poured a cup of coffee. He sat there a long time sipping the welcome brew, his mind searching for a reason why two men who seemed to be at odds with each other should be losing good sleeping time in whispered conversation.

Eventually however he tossed the dregs into the fire and rolled into his soogans. Jeff slightly loosened the red bandanna around his neck, a bandanna he never removed because it covered the scar that would stay with him forever. He also eased the thin black thong that hung around his throat and down the back of his neck. It carried a paper-thin knife in a soft doe-skin sheath. Hours of practice had made him an expert with the lethal blade that had so nearly taken his life. Last of all he checked his twin sixes. Satisfied, he closed his eyes and slipped into a sleep so finely balanced that the slightest wrong sound would bring him instantly into full awareness.

The next morning at breakfast Jeff noticed that McBride and Virgil Calder studiously avoided each other as usual so perhaps he had been mistaken, maybe it had been one of the Simes brothers. Jeff shrugged the thought aside as Wes strolled up to join the line.

'Mornin',' Jeff greeted, with a grin. 'How come you ain't first in the line today, fella? Ain't like you to be a tail-ender.'

'Maybe I ain't so hungry today,' responded Wes stiffly.

'Off your feed? That ain't like you, feller,' Jeff joked.

'*Some* things kin turn a man's stomach,' replied Calvin evenly, staring at Jeff. 'Other things kin make a body downright sour.'

Jeff realized that for some reason Wes was not his usual self. 'That supposed to mean something?' he questioned.

'Maybe so, maybe not; you figger it out,' snapped Wes, deliberately staring off towards the herd and totally ignoring Jeff.

'Come on, move it, cowboy, I ain't got all day,' groused the cook, as Jeff paused to question Wes further. 'Stick out your plate if you want breakfast or get out of line,' grumbled Killick.

Jeff collected his breakfast and made his way back to the fire to his usual group.

'Any idea what's gotten into Wes?' he asked as he sat down. 'Fella seems to have bedded down on a hornets' nest; 'bout as friendly as a rattler on a bad day.'

The men grunted and shrugged non-committally; no one seemed particularly talkative, at least not to him. Although a desultory conversation floated back and forth regarding the herd, the usual raillery was missing and Jeff could only assume that it was because they had entered Indian territory and the men were on edge.

This did not seem to apply to the other group, however. Normally a taciturn bunch at best, they seemed to be in good spirits this morning for some reason.

Feeling somehow out of things Jeff finished his breakfast and scoured his plate in sand before handing it back to the usually garrulous cook who took it with a monosyllabic grunt. Jeff was beginning to feel as if he was carrying a bad smell around.

'Have I upset somebody, Cookie?' he asked, perplexed.

'Trail boss comin',' grunted Killick. 'Probably lookin' fer you.'

'I want you to ride with me today, Mason,' Matt Tyler told him in that gravelly voice of his. 'Need two of us to watch out for the Comanche. An' you, Cookie, stay just ahead of the herd; don't go traipsin' too far ahead if y'all want to keep your hair, if that little bit is worth the keepin'.' Then he raised his voice to shout at McBride, 'You move up to point with Calvin; tell Pinter to take swing until we git back, OK?'

'Who's lead man?' queried McBride, half belligerently.

'Wes; an' I don't want any arguments, you hear me, McBride?'

'I hear you.'

'Good, let's ride, Mason.'

The two men mounted and rode out as the rest of the men dispersed to their chores.

Jeff and the trail boss rode stirrup to stirrup in total silence for some time before Matt Tyler opened the conversation. 'What was goin' on back there, Mason?'

'Search me, boss,' grunted Jeff. 'Beginning to think I'd got the plague or something.'

'Somethin' ain't right an' that's fer sure,' muttered Tyler. 'McBride bin keepin' his trap shut?'

'Seems so, at least I ain't heard anything.'

'You speak any Injun?' asked Tyler, abruptly changing the subject.

'Some.'

'OK for Comanch' then.'

'If they stop to listen.'

'Why shouldn't they?' asked Tyler.

'Would you? It's their country.'

'Yeah, well we haven't seen any Injuns yet.'

'Look yonderly over to the east in those foothills; there's two or three keepin' an eye on us,' replied Jeff quietly.

'The hell you say?'

'Bin dogging us for the last five or six miles. Maybe they figger to do a deal, cows in exchange for a clear passage; how'd you feel about that, Mr Tyler?'

'We're about to find out,' growled the trail boss. 'Looks like they want to parley. Wonder how many more there are hidden over there.'

The three Comanches rode slowly towards Jeff and his boss. Two were braves, single feathers knotted into their hair, lances pointing towards the sky. The third was a minor chieftain with three feathers fixed upright at the back of his head. He carried an ancient flintlock musket in the crook of one arm. The three stopped and waited, sitting upright on their mounts, their dignity and singleness of purpose obvious.

'If he fires that blunderbuss he'll probaby do us a favour by blowing all three of 'em to Hell,' muttered Tyler, as they slowed to a stop in front of the Indians.

'What do the Comanche warriors want with us that they trail us through the hills hiding their faces like snakes in the sand?' Tyler asked abruptly.

Jeff saw the warriors stiffen. 'You don't make friends easily do you, Mr Tyler,' he said wryly.

'Put 'em on the defensive right off, that's my way,' muttered Tyler.

'Don't look to be on the defensive to me, boss, they look about ready to cut our throats.'

'You cross our hunting grounds with your cattle; we need food until the buffalo comes.' The statement was flat and simple.

Tyler pasted a smile on his face. 'We will leave five animals after we've passed.' He held up one hand with the fingers splayed and carefully counted them off.

The Indians started muttering angrily; it was obvious to the two cowboys that this was not satisfactory. The Indian held up his hand also with his fingers splayed, then he opened and closed the hand five times.

'If they think I'm gonna pay twenty-five steers they can think again,' he muttered, still keeping the smile for the benefit of the Indians as his hand edged nearer the Walker Colt on his hip. The Indians though were watching the hand intently.

'Don't reckon there's any more of 'em around; we'd have seen 'em before this,' Tyler muttered. His head was still nodding up and down as if agreeing with the terms. He took the hand away from the holster and lifted it as if signalling final agreement before riding away. He part-turned his mount, concealing his weapon from the Comanches.

The Indians relaxed, obviously thinking the parley was over and the white men were about to ride away.

The salute over, Tyler dropped his hand. The Walker Colt came up in one smooth movement. The Indians didn't stand a chance.

Jeff's shout of anger was drowned in the thunder of the heavy gun as three bullets smashed into the unsuspecting Comanches knocking them from their mounts.

On the heels of the shots Jeff heard the thrum of galloping horses and the yip-yipping of Indian braves as six enraged Comanches erupted from a coulée where they had been hiding. This was no time to stop and argue. Turning his mustang on a dime Jeff used his spurs to drive his mount swiftly in the wake of the trail boss who was already heading for a jumble of boulders further up the trail.

Arrows were showering about the two men as they reached the shelter and dived for cover snatching their Winchesters from saddle-boots as they dismounted.

The two men lay beside each other panting from the sudden exertion.

'I thought you'd agreed with their terms,' panted Jeff. 'What the hell made you shoot 'em?'

'Agreed nothin'!' snarled Tyler. 'Twenty-five steers! Are you loco? That represents more'n six hundred bucks in Abilene, an' if we give in to these we'll have to go on paying all across the Indian Territories. Time we git to where we're headin' we'll have no steers left to sell.'

'This way we might not even get there,' replied Jeff succinctly. 'Right here just might be our last stopping place this side of Hell.'

There had been no sound or sight of the Indians since the two men had dived into cover so Tyler cautiously raised his head above the boulder to take a

look. Three arrows passed close enough to make him
duck back into its protection with a lurid curse.

'At least they don't seem to have any guns,' growled
the trail boss. 'We should be able to take care of half a
dozen Indians between us.'

'There was no need of this,' snapped Jeff. 'We
could have done a deal.'

'The only deal I'll make is with the stock yards in
Abilene,' retorted Tyler. 'Now, let's move around and
git these varmints before they get us.'

Jeff was angry that he had been dragged into an
unnecessary shoot-out with the Indians but he knew
that this was not the time for disputes, they were
pinned down and there was only one answer.
Someone had to die and Jeff did not intend that it
should be him.

Slipping from rock to rock he put distance between
himself and the trail boss who was already making his
presence felt. He counted four quick shots followed
by three more.

Jeff peered between some boulders. Two Indians
were making an attempt to cut around behind his
position. He fired a snapshot but missed. Jeff was
about to squeeze the trigger a second time when two
bullets spanged off the rock near his face making him
duck for cover, his eyes smarting from the particles of
stone.

The bullets had come from behind so he dropped
to the ground and squirmed around to face the
danger.

The gun spoke again and once more dust flew into
his face. In desperation Jeff powered to his feet
sending three rapid shots towards where he believed
his assailant was hiding as he dived for better cover.
There was no reply but he heard Matt Tyler

shouting, asking if he was OK. A few moments later the trail boss came lumbering through the rocks still calling for him.

Jeff poked his head above his hiding-place. 'Watch it, boss!' he shouted. 'One of 'em has a carbine.'

'Yeah? Well they've gone now!' replied Tyler, as he entered the tiny clearing. 'I managed to get three of 'em before they lit out. You OK?'

Jeff stepped cautiously into the clearing. 'Yeah, guess so. Thought you said they didn't have any guns.'

'I didn't see any. Did you?'

'Didn't have much time to look but one of 'em had a carbine, a modern one too judging by the rate of fire. I'd like to take a look, see if it's lying around anywhere.'

'Be long gone by this time, and so should we,' replied Tyler. 'Don't think we've got any time fer sight-seein'; those war-whoops could be back with their pals. C'mon, let's ride.'

'I'd still like to look,' grunted Jeff.'

'I *said* we ride, now let's *do* it,' snapped Tyler, anger building in his voice as he turned away to look for his horse leaving Jeff arguing with himself.

There was virtually no conversation on the ride back to the herd; Tyler seemed happy to keep a brooding silence between them and Jeff still seethed at the way Tyler had placed both their lives in jeopardy for no apparent reason.

It almost seemed as if the trail boss wanted an excuse to kill Indians, yet he had to bring the herd through this territory. There was a lot of ground to cover before they reached the Kansas border and Tyler had just put a big wooden spoon in a pot that was already bubbling over with trouble.

Jeff absently pushed his hand into the pocket of his duster expecting to feel the Ranger badge. It was not there. Puzzled, he explored the other pocket and was momentarily reassured by its presence. A quick frown flitted across his face. The badge had been in his right-hand pocket, now it was in the left one, but he could not remember changing it.

After thinking about it some more he gave a mental shrug; maybe he had swapped it around while riding night herd. He had developed a habit of twisting and turning the badge between his fingers the way he'd once seen a gambler play with a silver dollar so perhaps he was mistaken.

The dust of the herd could be seen in the distance now and the two men kicked their mounts into a lope.

'Take over the point, Mason,' Tyler shouted, above the din. 'Keep 'em movin' towards that stand of rocks. We'll search for water ahead while the men stop to eat. I'll ride around an' warn the men to be on the look-out for war-whoops.'

Jeff nodded and turned into the herd signalling McBride to take up his position at swing, then he moved across to Wesley.

'Hi,' he greeted. 'We'd best keep our eyes peeled; we had a run-in with some Comanches up ahead.'

The black man did not acknowledge the greeting and merely nodded agreement in response to the information.

'What's with you, Wes?' asked Jeff, anger and irritation pulling at him. 'Have I done somethin'?'

'Nope,' grunted Wesley succinctly. 'Just mindin' my business is all.'

'I thought we were friends.'

'So did I,' replied Wes.

'So what's happened to make it different?'

'Let it lay.'

'Like to know, Wes,' replied Jeff. 'We started OK didn't we?'

'I thought so.'

'So what happened?'

'I said, let it lay,' replied Wes, staring stoically ahead.

Jeff rode a short distance beside the black man hoping he'd open up and explain, but when he realized that he was getting nowhere Jeff eased across to his position at point and rode in disconsolate silence.

He'd enjoyed his friendship with Wes and he had no idea what had soured it; maybe things would get straightened out as the herd moved on. He sure hoped so; the drive had been nothing but trouble so far.

FOUR

The second river crossing was made without much trouble; according to the trail boss someone had named it The Canadian. They were four weeks into Indian Territory now and although the Indians were still out there, so far they had kept their distance.

As they left the river behind, the dryness and dust took over again. The sun rose like a brass ball in the sky and even at night there was no let-up. The stifling heat was making the steers more restless by the hour. The trail boss had managed to find a small amount of water at the last two stops but as dusk closed in the trail boss returned with the news that the herd would have a dry camp.

'Keep 'em moving in as tight a circle as possible, boys,' growled Tyler in that gravelly voice of his as heat lightning flashed in the sky. 'This 'un could be nasty, no unsaddling and the watch is doubled. Come in fer grub in twos, the rest keep at it until they settle down.'

Gradually the night darkened but there was no respite. The sticky cloying heat seemed to suffocate a man and the lightning continued to flash across the sky followed by faint rumbles of thunder, all adding to the cattle's unease. Once again there was a tingle of static in the air making nerves taut with expectancy.

The feel of danger showed in the plaintive lowing of the beeves, the nervous twitch of the horses' ears, a restlessness transferring itself from man to beast.

Jeff was on the midnight watch with Sam Pinter, Quincy McBride and Bart Simes. They were following each other around the herd singing softly, reassuring the steers by their calm presence as the lightning headed closer and the thunder-heads built up blotting out the moon.

Suddenly there was a terrific clap of thunder followed almost instantly by a bolt of lightning. It zig-zagged from the sky like a writhing finger directly into the herd dancing across the horns of the frantic animals like a whirling dervish, creating havoc as it flashed again and again from one frightened animal to the next.

Instantly the steers were up and running, bursting from the circle with a deafening bellow of fear. From the camp Jeff faintly heard the frantic cry of *stampede*!

The run started just ahead of him heading directly for the camp. He fed spurs to his mount in an attempt to keep the maddened beasts from breaking out.

Jeff was just beginning to make a slight impression on the leaders when he heard three rapid gunshots.

The cattle were beyond control as they leaned into the horse and rider. Jeff was compelled to run with the herd to avoid being forced into the mêlée where his mount could easily lose its footing or be gored by one of the deadly horns. Nothing could save a man if he were to fall into the path of a stampede.

Leaning along the racing mustang's neck Jeff rode with consummate skill giving the animal every possible chance to ease into the herd in an attempt to force it to turn.

The camp loomed ahead, devastated by the maddened beasts. The chuck wagon was on its side and he glimpsed Ward Killick clinging desperately to a wheel as the cattle surged around and past it. Jeff found himself hoping the old man would make it in spite of the odds.

From the corner of his eye he saw one of the young lads turn his horse into the stampede, trying to ride against it. For a moment he managed to stay upright but then he was whisked into the maelstrom to be trampled underfoot.

Jeff rode on using every trick he knew to stay in the saddle and keep up with the herd. Then the sky seemed to burst apart as rain poured in a torrent.

The herd gradually slowed in the face of the downpour, the stampede breaking down. At last Jeff managed to gain ground on the leaders and began to push them into the beginnings of a turn.

He straightened up, knowing that it was almost over when a shadow appeared out of the gloom behind him. Jeff felt a terrific thump on his back somersaulting him over his mount's head, shoulder crashing into the side of one of the steers as he fell.

By sheer chance the force of the blow bounced him out of the cattle run where he lay unconscious, his body within inches of those deadly hooves as the steers thundered past....

Jeff blinked and slowly opened mud-caked eyes, his back and legs a mass of pain. The rain still teemed down and he was bone cold. As he slipped again into semi-consciousness, his eyes registered that it was dawn and his mind tried to search for a reason why he had not been found. The effort was too much and unconsciousness claimed him. He came to as the rain stopped and he could feel the welcome warmth of the sun on his back. There were voices as if from a great distance and his first instinct was to try to call for help but something made him pause as he forced his mind to focus on the voices.

McBride's seemed to be the dominant voice, almost as if he were in charge.

'That's the end of him I reckon.'

A hand pressed into his neck. 'There's a pulse, he ain't dead yet.'

That voice sounded like one of the Simes brothers.

'D'you want to put a bullet in him, Wes?' asked McBride.

'Leave it. Be more natural if anybody finds him. He'll be dead in a few hours anyway, killed in the stampede.'

That was Matt Tyler, but why would they want to kill him? Jeff asked himself.

A foot pushed cruelly into his damaged shoulder almost forcing a groan from him but he managed to stifle it.

'That was some whack you fetched him, McBride,' grunted Tyler. 'Must've broke his back I reckon.'

'Hope I did,' snarled McBride. 'Threatened to pull a gun on me, the bastard.'

'Shall I put a slug in 'im then?' asked another voice Jeff could not recognize.

'Nah,' replied McBride. 'Let 'im die like Matt said. Hope he suffers first though.'

The voices began to fade as the men walked away. Jeff vaguely heard someone say that perhaps the Indians would find him.

Slowly his mind began to blank out. He could not understand what had happened or why the men all seemed set on leaving him behind, but somewhere deep inside, Jeff knew they'd made a big mistake. His body relaxed and he slept as the mud caked and dried on his heavy coat.

FIVE

The morning broke bright and clear after the storm and the men were busy rounding up the longhorns until well past noon.

Quincy McBride jogged his pony over to the shattered chuck wagon and began to collect whatever stores he could find.

Dispassionately he stared at the still figure of Ward Killick lying in a limp bundle beneath the pile of wood that had been the floor of the wagon. He started to ease his gun from his holster with obvious intent, then shrugged as he looked up and saw Matt Tyler standing beside him shaking his head.

'He's an old man,' grunted Tyler. 'He ain't gonna last more than a few hours in this heat anyway. If anyone should come along they'll find him an' Mason. Look kinda natural, Indian raid an' stampede, no bullets to give the game away.'

'Yeah, that's about the right of it,' agreed McBride. 'What about the others?'

'There's only Calvin Calder an' Billy-Joe. I don't figure Calvin will cause us a problem; he's afraid of the Texas Ranger. Reckon Calder ain't no better than the rest of us, but it leaves a lot to share the take with.'

McBride grinned. 'We need 'em all now, to see the herd through Indian territory. As long as we keep 'em sweet till we git to where we're goin', we kin give 'em their share out of a six-gun. One bullet apiece should do it.'

'Yeah,' replied Tyler doubtfully. 'But you ain't the boss of this little shindig. Have you got his word on this? Just who is he anyway?'

'Don't git curious on me, Tyler,' growled Quincy McBride. 'I'm running this show an' you got *my* word on it. There's gonna be just five in the final split, me, you an' the Simes brothers ... if they live long enough to collect....'

'That's only four,' interrupted Tyler.

'D'you suppose the head man is doin' this for free?' snapped McBride testily. 'Now remember, you're still the trail boss so git everybody movin'. I'll load the other wagon with what grub I kin find in this mess an' let's get away from here. You go on treatin' me like somethin' nasty on the bottom of your boot, like you've bin doin' all along.' His voice dropped to a threatening growl. 'But don't git curious, Tyler, otherwise the number in the share-out could be reduced by one, *comprende?*'

Tyler dragged his mount around without a word. This was the second time McBride had shown his authority over him. He'd done it back there where Mason was lying injured in the mud. Tyler knew he would have to get back to the top of the heap. Every cow waddy on the drive expected him to be in charge and by God he'd make sure they saw him that way.

For the next two hours Matt Tyler was everywhere, shouting and cajoling, pushing the men into greater efforts to get the herd moving.

Eventually the cattle were strung out along the trail heading away from the scene of the stampede.

Tyler watched in quiet satisfaction as the herd

slowly pushed along in an orderly line with Quincy
McBride and Wesley Calvin riding point, Carl Simes
riding swing and Virgil Calder on the flank.

Bart Simes and Sam Pinter moved between the
drag and flank to help Billy-Joe and Seth Calhoun
keep the drag and remuda up tight leaving as few
stragglers as possible.

The whole crew knew that with their reduced
numbers, the Indians would quickly round up any
stragglers that wandered too far away from the main
herd and they would very soon realize that there
would be no cowboys to spare to try to recapture the
strays.

As the last of the herd swept past, Matt Tyler stared
through the dust at the desolate-looking camp-site,
the chuck wagon, smashed almost to a pulp with one
shaft sticking up in the air like an accusing finger
pointing towards the brassy sky, the broken timbers
covering the body of the elderly cook.

His eyes flipped over to where a mud-covered
mound marked the body of Mason, the Texas
Ranger.

Two of the three men who represented the owners
of the cattle plodding up the trail were gone. The
only other one was Sam Pinter, and he'd probably be
next unless he toed the line.

Matt Tyler heaved a sigh, partly of regret as he
took one last look before turning his pony and loping
towards the front of the herd.

He had planned to bring many more herds along
this trail. Had visions of becoming a legend on the
Chisholm Trail but the lure of quick wealth had
smothered his ambitions and he had become a
rustler.

Tyler shrugged off his melancholy throughts as he

pushed his mount into a faster pace. He had to find water before nightfall or McBride would be kicking his ass.

Tyler's mouth tightened at the thought. If anyone had told him that he would ever be taking orders from a loud-mouthed deserter like McBride he'd have laughed in their face, but he wasn't laughing now. He was taking orders from a man so stupid that he had wanted to shoot Mason and Killick for his own gratification, not caring that he would be leaving clear evidence behind for others to find.

'I'll be damned glad when this drive is over and I've got my share of the beef money stashed safely in my jeans,' Tyler muttered. 'Don't trust McBride or his boss no further than I can throw a full-growed bull buffalo with one hand.'

Gradually the site of the stampede fell further and further behind as they headed towards the North Canadian river.

Matt Tyler's lip curled in contempt when he thought of McBride. True he didn't know who McBride's boss was, but one thing was sure: once they left the great brown trail made by Jesse Chisholm's cattle, the whole crew would be lost.

Only he had made it a point to find out everything he could about the Indian Territories. He'd heard of the North Canadian and the Cimarron rivers from others who had travelled from Kansas through to Texas. His plan was to ease away from the trail after crossing the Cimarron and cut towards Salt Fork. Matt figured that he could hold the cattle close to the river there while they were rebranded.

His lip curled again. The whole shooting match depended on him so McBride had better watch himself; it didn't pay to get too uppity in the middle of the Territories.

Tyler glanced over his shoulder, the herd was moving along nicely now. What was done was done; Mason had seemed a nice enough feller ... till he'd seen the badge. Pity about the old man, but he never would have gone along with the steal anyway. The sun rose and set on the Circle C-connected as far as Killick was concerned.

Tyler shrugged again as he settled in the saddle. He'd made his choice so there was nothing left but to stick with it.

SIX

When Jeff next opened his eyes it was early evening, his body still throbbing with pain. He knew he had to move or become prey to a predator, animal or human.

His body was raging with thirst and only the mud thrown over him by the stampeding longhorns had protected him from the heat of the day. Slowly, inch by inch, he began to move his hands and arms, the dried mud crackling as it fell away from his coat.

While he had slept his body had been repairing itself. The pain was bad, but not as bad as it had been. Slowly, agonizingly, he forced himself to stand. His head went into a spin and he almost collapsed as his stomach did a flip-flop.

Standing with legs braced apart slowly he looked around. There was no sign of the herd. Jeff tried to focus on the horizon. It was empty so the outfit had to be miles away. He looked back over his shoulder to where the camp had been and winced as pain seared through his back and shoulder.

The remains of the chuck wagon with one shaft pointing towards the sky caught his eye, triggering a faint hope that some of the goods originally stored in the wagon might still be there.

Concentrating with every fibre, Jeff forced himself

to put one foot in front of the other as pain screamed along his back in protest.

Cracked and bruised lips, damaged in the fall, were forced into a parody of a smile. 'If you think you've stopped me, McBride, think again,' he gritted. 'It's a long way to Abilene, mister, but believe me, I'll be there!'

The effort had taken all Jeff's reserves, and he leaned against the side of the shattered wagon for support.

The ominous click of a gun going on to full cock and the business end of a pistol being pushed into his stomach drove the tiredness out of him in a second.

'Kin you think of one goddamned reason why I shouldn't blow you all to Hell?' husked a tired old voice.

Jeff allowed himself to relax a little. 'Left you behind as well did they, old-timer?'

'I ain't so damned old, nor stupid neither,' grumbled Killick. 'You so much as blink an' you're dead.'

'You got anything to eat or drink in that beat-up old chuck wagon, Ward?'

'An' what if I have? Y'all gonna help me eat it I suppose!'

'Like to, old-timer.'

'Just damn-well bet you would,' grumbled Killick. 'An' don't call me old-timer. Name's Ward or Killick. Who might you be, mister? Cain't see fer all that mud.'

'Mason.'

'Oh yeah, Ranger Jeff Mason ain't it?'

'I ain't a ranger. Well, not exactly.'

'You gotta badge; seen it, McBride showed it tuh me.'

'I was just carryin' it for a friend. We gonna jaw all day or do I get a drink?'

The gun was withdrawn and Jeff sank slowly on to his buttocks as the old man passed him a rather dented tin mug. The water tasted wonderful. He passed the mug back and the old man refilled it. Jeff drank the second one pausing to savour it. 'Good water,' he muttered gratefully as he returned the mug.

'Ain't so bad,' agreed Killick grudgingly. 'There's bits where you have to chew but once y'all git it down it ain't bad at all.'

'You any idea what the hell's going on here?' Jeff asked.

'Search me,' replied the old man. 'At first I thought they were gonna snatch the herd. You seen anythin' of Sam Pinter?'

'Nope, but then I ain't bin in the mood for sight-seeing so far today.'

'But iffen he was around we'd have heard from him by this time,' grumbled Ward.

'Unless he's dead; I was only a whisker away from turning up dead myself,' replied Jeff.

Ward Killick crawled from beneath the wagon where he had been hiding, seemingly as spry as ever.

'There's several bits an' pieces under there. You have a bite to eat an' I'll take a look-see.'

'Watch out for Indians, Ward,' Jeff called, as he grubbed under the wagon and came up clutching a large chunk of mud-covered bread which he attempted to brush off on an equally muddy coat before taking a healthy bite.

It was over an hour later when Ward Killick slid beneath the wagon carrying two rifles.

'Nothin' else out there except a splatter of blood an'

bones. One of the younkers trampled in the stampede unless I miss my guess,' he reported. 'Found these on two dead nags; thought they might come in handy. One was your mustang with the yaller blaze on his foreleg, t'other was just a mess of bones. No spare bullets though, still, might come in handy, huh?'

'Yeah, that's mine,' replied Jeff, taking the rifle and checking that the magazine was full. 'I've got some spare shells in my belt, not many but it's better than nothin'. Somebody must have taken my pistols while I was out of it, damn their thievin' souls.'

'Reckon we ought to spend a couple of days here before movin' on, give you time to get rid of your aches an' pains,' grumbled Ward Killick. 'I just cain't let 'em get away with my young boss's cows an' that's flat.'

'Me neither,' growled Jeff. 'I managed to dig out some grub while you were gone. If only we had some broncs we'd damn soon catch up with 'em.' Jeff grimaced as he tried to move too quickly. 'You're right, pardner. I ain't gonna be able to walk too good for the next couple of days so we'd best keep out of sight and hope the Indians keep following the herd.'

The two men slept fitfully that night in their cold camp under the overturned wagon, waiting for full daylight before kindling an almost smokeless fire. While Jeff kept a watch for marauding Indians, Ward Killick brewed some coffee and cooked some bacon and beans. Both men tucked into the fare with gusto, savouring the warmth of the fire until it burnt out.

With nothing to do but keep out of sight and watch, Jeff told Ward Killick about himself and Nathaniel Kyle and what good friends they had become. 'So, I'm following that herd to hell and back if I have to,' Jeff finished.

'I'm with you all the way,' grunted Killick in that high-pitched moaning voice of his. 'I work for *the* most gutsy young feller you ever saw, nobody could push him no matter what. I want you tuh promise me that iffen I don't make it you'll make sure he gits his *dinero*.' The old man stared at Jeff, his eyes pleading for understanding. 'This youngster took everythin' anybody tried to throw at him an' still beat the odds, by God. Like to tell yuh about him iffen you've got the time.'

'We've sure got plenty of that,' replied Jeff. 'Always supposing the Indians leave us in peace.'

'You asked fer it, so here goes,' said Killick with a sad smile. 'It all started about three years back just afore the end of the war. Carpetbaggers was movin' in everywhere, takin' over land, crops an' such, working the proper owners out by killin' or stealin' then they'd git legal bits of paper from Washington to take over ground that farmers and ranchers had bin usin' fer years. They were gitting rich hand over fist. I saw women an' kids kicked off farms their daddy had sweated over for years, their pa almost always turned up dead just before the carpetbaggers took over.

'Well, mister, I'm tellin' you, they made a mistake about this youngster. Yessir, a hell'uva big mistake. That's when I found out that some people just won't be pushed. They laughed at him but he sure-God showed 'em.

'I'd come out of the army an' was just loafin' around like, waiting for work to come and find me. Well, it didn't take me long to size up what was happenin' in that little one-hoss town. Feller by the name of Len Gratton had the place by the throat, marshal an' all. He already had a sizeable slice of the country in his pocket but he wanted more. Fact is he wanted it all.

'He'd find a rancher who'd bin runnin' a spread fer years but who didn't have any real title to all the land, then he'd either run 'em into a gambling debt or give 'em a mortgage on the bits of property they did own. Next thing you know the *hombre* would turn up dead an' Gratton would foreclose, gettin' the land fer next to nothin'.

'Well, sir, Jason Case was one of these fellers; he'd bin the first in the valley an' his spread was *the* best. Now it just stood to reason that sooner or later the damned carpetbagger was gonna covet that piece of land an' it also stood to reason that big Jason wasn't about to let him have it. No one will ever know just what would have happened if fancy-pants Len Gratton an' that old bull elk, Jason Case had locked horns because Jason was fetched in one mornin' face down across his saddle. He was *supposed* to have taken a fall an' busted his skull, which was nonsense because Jason was safer on his bronc than most people were in a rockin'-chair.

'Well, they all tut-tutted an' said how sorry they was, but it stuck out a country mile who was responsible. An' the damned thief didn't waste any time neither. No sooner was old Jason under the sod than Gratton started shovin'. He sent a gang of gunnies to the Circle C-connected an' told Ma Case to pack up an' git. Young Johnny Case kicked up one hell'uva fuss an' two bully boys worked him over just fer the hell of it. Brother was *that* a mistake.'

'Who was Johnny Case,' asked Jeff, intrigued by the tale, 'old Jason's brother?'

'Young Johnny? He's my boss. Jason's son. No-but thirteen he was then but big with it, quiet lad an' a hard worker. He knew in his own mind who was responsible fer his old man's death an' he told the gunnies so straight out. But he was just a kid so they kicked his ass an' told his ma to be long gone by sundown. Then they rode back to town with Sandy Miller leadin'. He was the *segundo,* tough an' quick with his guns too. Anyway, he went back to town, told his boss that the ranch was sure to be clear by sundown, then wandered into the saloon to crow a little.'

'What about young Johnny?' prodded Jeff as Killick drifted into silence, obviously reliving the past.

'I tell yuh Jeff, that lad had taken the beatin' of a lifetime an' he sure took some patchin' up, but his ma was up to it. Then she turned to start packin'. "We ain't goin' no place, Ma", Johnny told her. "I'm about to cut them *hombres* down to size". Well, 'pears his ma begged an' pleaded with him. "They'll shoot you down", she told him, but it made no difference to the youngster. He saddled up his daddy's hoss, picked up his old man's Greener an' a pocketful of cartridges then loped off into town.

'I was there, sitting on the boardwalk, still waitin' fer work tuh turn up, when young Johnny rode in. All battered up like he was the lad sure didn't look ready to buck the tiger to me. No sir!'

'So what happened?' asked Jeff getting exasperated by Ward's slow way of telling the tale.

'I'm gittin' there. Who's doin' the tellin' here?' grumbled Killick. 'Anyway, first off Johnny spots one of the men who had bin in the gang out at the ranch. "Hey you", he calls, "where-at do I find Sandy Miller?" The guy grins kinda sarcastic like. "Run along home sonny", he laughs. "Iffen Sandy catches sight of you he'll kick your ass again".

'Wa-al now the kid tilts that old Greener so the guy was lookin' right down the barrels; it must have

looked like the gates of Hell 'cos he went an awful
funny colour.

' "I asked yuh a question *hombre*", answered
Johnny, kinda polite-like. Because he was a very
polite young feller as you kin tell.

' "He-he's in the saloon", stuttered the tough boy.

' "Thank yuh kindly", replied the kid. "You kin go
fer your iron now". While the tough boy was thinkin'
about this piece of news the kid trips the hammer an'
damn-near cuts the *hombre* in half, an' that old hoss
didn't even twitch. Then he flips out the spent
cartridge an' rams in a fresh one. Turns his daddy's
old grey mare around an' plods right on down the
road to the saloon.

'Now I know a Greener goin' off makes one
hell'uva din but guns weren't new so nobody took
much notice at the time ... but they should have.
Anyhow, young Johnny un-ships at the saloon an'
pushes inside. Sandy Miller was at the bar with a
crowd of his pals, tellin' 'em how he'd scared the hell
out of Ma Case an' how he'd beaten the shit out of the
kid. Most of the *hombres* moved out of the way kinda
fast when they felt the kid's Greener pushin' 'em in
the back an' the lad kept goin' until the shotgun was
tickling Sandy Miller's backbone.

' "I'd kinda like y-all to turn around, slowish if
yuh please, Mister Miller", the kid told him, all
respectful like. Well, Miller kinda stiffened up an'
turned around, real slow. "What's this all about
sonny?" growled Miller, like he was in a bad temper
or somethin'. "Nobody pushes a gun in my back".'

' "Just fer the record, suh, I'd like to know if Mister
Gratton ordered you to hooraw Ma an' me at the
ranch", the kid said, calm as you please.

' "So what if it was?" asked Gratton, real nasty like.

"You figger to do somethin' about it?"

' "Why, yes sir, I surely do", replied the kid, tiltin' that ol' Greener so that Miller could take a good look down the barrels like that other feller had. "I'm gonna count to three, Mister Miller suh. You kin go fer your iron any time you like 'cos I'm gonna blow your damned head off". See what a real polite kid he was? Miller was one tough cookie, Jeff, but one look at that Greener an' his tan kinda faded leavin' him as white as a fresh laundered sheet.

' "When you're ready Mister Miller", Johnny told him. "I'll count up to three. One, two" *Bang!* an' Miller was spread all over the bar. Wa-al, Jeff, he just punched out the cartridge like he did that last time, an' marched out. As a man there weren't much of him, but in my book he was ten feet tall an' twice as wide. That was when the marshal stepped into the road, holdin' his hand up all important-like. "Hold on, son", he said, kinda stern. "I wanna know just what went on in there".

'The kid didn't say a word, just tilted that old Greener an' fer a minute there I thought the marshal was gonna git his last peek down the barrel. An' he must have thought so too 'cos he stopped dead in his tracks.

' "Just turn around an' walk ahead of me", ordered young Johnny, "an' if any of your deputies try to interfere, you are one gone marshal. You understand me, mister?" Well, son, as God's my judge, we all marched down to that big house of Gratton's an' there he was, on the front porch with a gun-hung *hombre* either side of him.

' "What the hell's all this I bin hearin'?" he yells as Johnny gets to the gate. The kid pushes the marshal aside with the shot-gun an' Gratton gets to see the

Greener for the first time. Which makes him set back
a little I kin tell you.

' "Understand you sent some men to have Ma an'
me kicked off our ranch, Mister Gratton, that so?"

' "That's so", agreed Gratton. "You don't have
deeds to that land".

' "Ain't that the pure truth", agreed young Johnny.
"But what I'd like tu know is, have *you* got this here
deed right now?"

' "I will have by morning", sneers Gratton, real
sassy.

' "So if you ain't got this here deed, an' I ain't got it
then you don't have any more right to the land than I
do, ain't that so, Mister Gratton?" the kid asks.

' "That's right, sonny, it goes to the man who can
hold it, an' that's *me*, fella", Gratton said, smilin' all
around like there weren't any doubts about it.

' "No it ain't", replied the kid. "That's *me*, an' this
Greener says so".

' "I got two gunnies siding me right here an' there's
plenty more, so why don't you get some sense an'
move on, sonny, afore I kick your ass", the feller told
the boy.

' "Y'all ain't got nobody, Mister Gratton sir", the kid
told him. "I can't see those two men standing beside
you when you die 'cos they'll die also, and even if one
of 'em lived, who'd pay him? Now I'm askin' you
fellers real nice", the kid told 'em, "you stayin' or
leavin'?"

'Well sir, I'm tellin' you, those two gunnies undid
their gunbelts an' left. Stepping real careful, like they
was walking on glass or somethin'.

' "See what I mean, Mister Gratton?" young Johnny
told him. "This is *your* day to be pushed so you just
drag iron any time you're ready".

'Well, we could all see Gratton was desperate; he
started to back off holding his hands in front of him.
"Easy son", he muttered, like he had a job swallerin'.
"I ain't drawing, see, my hands are up".

'The hammers of the Greener clicked on to full
cock. "One more step an' you're dead", the kid told
him quietly. "There's no way out, so draw, Mister
Gratton suh, *draw*".

'An' Gratton tried. God how he tried. He got his
guns half-clear before the kid gave him both barrels
an' plastered him all over his grand front porch.
Then the kid just turned around and walked back to
his hoss, climbed aboard and jogged along main
street.

'I touched my hat to 'im in a kinda salute; showin'
my respect, and he nodded. "You feel like ridin' fer a
spread bein' run by a bit of a kid, mister?" he asked
me. Real serious he was.

' "Don't mind if I do," I told him.

' "Git your bronc an' ride out to the Circle
C-connected when you've a mind to", he said, and
then he just rode out of town.'

There was a long pause as the old man sat there
contemplating, and Jeff stared out into the waning
sunlight searching for any sign of trouble.

'You kin see why I just gotta make sure young
Johnny Case gits his *dinero*, Jeff. Things is tough on
the range, you know that, an' a spunky kid like
Johnny deserves to beat the odds once in a while.'

There was a pleading note in his voice again. 'If I
don't make it, will you do your damnedest to try to get
that dough back to young Johnny?'

'I could say yes, and still keep it for myself,
old-timer.'

'Don't reckon you would though.'

'Why?'

'You're a bit like young Johnny, you'll do what's right come hell or high water, I feel it in my bones.'

'OK, you got my word on it.'

'Thanks, son, I wanna say....'

'Let's pack up what grub we've found and move out, it's getting dark,' interrupted Jeff brusquely, knowing how much it would cost Ward to lower his pride. 'The further we can get before daylight the better, so let's rattle our hocks, huh?'

Ward Killick grinned his relief as he scurried about under the wagon wrapping the bits of food in pieces of torn canvas ripped from the roof of the ruined wagon and stuffing them inside his shirt.

Night was closing in fast by the time they had stowed the food about their bodies. They had also managed to save two canteens of water from the bottom of the water barrel which had not quite overturned when the wagon had capsized in the stampede.

They collected their rifles and crawled cautiously from their hiding-place. Both knew that they would have about an hour before the moon cut into the inky blackness, so the further they were from the wagon when that happened, the better.

They would have no trouble following the herd, the way ahead was clearly marked in a wide brown swathe where a total of over 12,000 hooves had cut into the grass over the last few months.

It was a slow start; Jeff's body protested strongly at first but gradually his muscles limbered up and he began to increase the pace.

Ward Killick moved on uncomplainingly at his side and Jeff was surprised at the elderly man's endurance.

When the big round moon crept into the sky both men increased their vigilance; it was a popular belief that Indians did not attack at night, but neither Jeff nor his companion were about to bet their lives on it.

They continued on throughout the night in companionable silence but as the light of the moon began to wane they headed for the foothills to the left of the tracks.

Having found a suitable niche in the rocks they lit a small fire and cooked some bacon liberally laced with mud, and even managed some coffee before dousing the fire and settling down.

'Figger to stay here until dark,' Jeff mumbled around a chunk of bacon.

'Makes sense,' agreed Ward. 'Coffee ain't bad.'

'The mud don't do much for the flavour,' grunted Jeff.

'You're sure gettin' picky; afore you met me you didn't have anythin'.'

'So boast about it,' grunted Jeff as he tossed away the dregs and lay back. 'You can do the first three hours.'

'Thanks very much,' moaned Ward. 'Who made you the boss of this outfit?'

'I did; you're too old.'

'Huh, if I left you behind you'd git lost, young feller,' grunted Ward as he settled down to take the first watch. 'Bet it's nice to have somebody real reliable around to wipe your nose for yuh; damn youngsters today got no respect....'

His grumbling was answered by a quiet snore.

SEVEN

Five gruelling days had passed. Jeff Mason and Ward Killick were putting one foot in front of the other by memory alone, their boots, never intended for walking anyway, were about worn out. Although Jeff had managed to kill a small deer they hadn't been allowed to eat it.

The shot had gained them the unwelcome attention of a band of roving Mescalero Apaches and they'd expended most of their ammunition fighting a rearguard action. Judging by what Jeff had discovered from Matt Tyler they were between a rock and a hard place.

They could live off the land if the Indians left them alone, but if Tyler had it right there were Mescaleros to their left, Kiowa Apaches on their right, with Southern Cheyenne and full-blood Kiowas ahead. As if that wasn't enough there was always the Comanche behind them just in case it got lonesome.

With 3,000 head of cattle and twelve men, all mounted and with guns for protection, travelling across this territory was dangerous. Two men on foot, half starved and short of water, was just a step short of suicide.

Jeff licked his cracked lips as he glanced sideways at his companion. 'Helluva country,' he husked.

'I've seen worse.' Ward stumbled, but pulled himself up and pressed on. 'Reckon we need some water real soon, son.'

'Yeah, well, Matt told me that there's a river up ahead somewheres called the North Canadian.'

'We passed that 'un,' muttered Ward, trying to spit without success.

'No, that was the Canadian, this un's the *North* Canadian.'

'Different, huh?'

'Yep.'

'The guy who named it sure had an active imagination.'

'I think I've got imagination also,' grunted Jeff, pointing ahead. 'That look like a river to you, Ward?'

'Ain't imagination, son,' agreed Ward, trying to spit and making it. 'That's water, sure as hell.'

Both men instinctively quickened their pace and almost ran the last few yards, stumbling into the water and falling on their faces, allowing themselves to be engulfed in the welcome coolness of the river.

They burst to the surface together, laughing and splashing, swishing the water over themselves, revelling in the feel of it, cleaning and cooling their bodies, before sinking below the surface once more.

A few seconds later they exploded to the surface again, but now both men were staring at the river bank where over a dozen Mescalero Apaches sat their mounts, watching and waiting.

Too late Jeff realized that he had allowed himself to be seduced into carelessness by the attraction of the water.

'Reckon we've found ourselves a problem, Ward,' he muttered.

'In spades,' grunted Killick. 'You speak 'Pache?'

Jeff raised his head, palm outwards in the sign of peace. 'Greetings! Kitchi Manito is good to provide water for the land and for the thirsty. Come, share it with us.'

'You speak our tongue?' questioned one, obviously a minor chieftain.

'It is an honour; I have lived with your people,' Jeff lied; he knew he could not mention his friendship with the Sioux who were sworn enemies of the Apache.

Two of the braves slipped from their ponies and collected the rifles Jeff and Ward had dropped in their rush for the water.

'You are friends of the Apache?' questioned the leader dubiously.

'We are both friends of the Apache,' Jeff replied, waving a hand to include Ward Killick.

'Yet you killed some of our braves when we came upon you in the hills. Why did you do this if you are our friends?'

Belatedly Jeff realized that it was the same band who had robbed them of their kill.

'You came upon us suddenly; we wished you no harm but you attacked us.'

'We will take you to our chief; the council will decide,' grunted the chieftain.

Four braves dismounted and splashed through the water, grabbed Jeff and Ward by the arms and propelled them towards the bank. The rifles were placed across their shoulders and their wrists were lashed to them. A brave dropped a noosed rope around each man's neck.

'If the council decides that you live, you will be freed, if not, you will die.' The chieftain turned his mount away from the two captives and moved off at a fast walking pace.

The rope around the two men's necks tightened as they trotted to keep up. Each knew that if they should fall it would be the end.

'Reckon I'm gonna have to call on you to keep your promise, Mason,' grumbled Ward. 'Don't think I'm up to all this exercise.'

'We'll make it, pardner,' replied Jeff grimly. 'Keep remembering how Tyler an' the rest left us to die.'

'It's gonna take more'n that, Jeff. I'm about done,' mumbled the old man as he stumbled and only just managed to retain his balance. 'Don't fergit, son, you promised!'

'I'll keep it if I can, old-timer.'

'That's good enough for me,' replied Ward in a strangled gasp. 'So long friend.'

Ward Killick stumbled a second time, tried to make it but failed. His toes kicked stubbornly at the dry earth as they dragged him along, choking him to death....

Matt Tyler was returning from a three-day scouting trip along the Cimarron River. He intended to leave the well-marked trail blazed by Jesse Chisholm and follow the river back to the closest point between the Cimarron and the Salt Fork of the Arkansas River, the place he had been told of by a frontiersman. This was rough, almost uncharted territory and Tyler was reluctant to leave the safety of the Cimarron until he had to.

The herd could not last long without water, and with his reduced crew, any idea of holding a stampede of thirst-crazed beeves in check was a waste of time. There was also the worry of Indian attacks. At least with the water on one side it would be easier to hold the cattle if the Indians did decide to attack the herd.

He was jolted out of his ruminations as he approachd the camp by voices raised in argument.

Matt Tyler sighed as he kicked his mount into a lope. One voice he knew well was raised above the others: Quincy McBride.

He entered the clearing in a swirl of dust, putting his mount squarely between McBride and Wesley Calvin.

'What the hell's goin' on here?' he growled. 'Can't I leave you two together fer a few days without one of you causing trouble? And what's the matter with you, Pinter? I left you in charge while I was gone.'

Sam Pinter waved a deprecating hand. 'That's all very well, Tyler,' he replied, in a surly tone, 'but if these two *hombres* are set to blow each other to hell I ain't about to try an' stop 'em. I'm here to watch out for my employer's interests. There's a thousand head of cattle belonging to the Lazy P, out there, so I ain't about to step between a pair of wildcats; it ain't part of the job.'

Tyler swung out of the saddle and stared belligerently at Pinter. 'I put you in charge while I was away. It was up to you to put a stop to this nonsense before it got started.'

Tyler inadvertently allowed his hand to drop to his pistol.

Pinter tensed and flexed his fingers. 'Don't start somethin' you can't finish, mister,' he warned.

Tyler felt a sudden coldness in the pit of his stomach; he hadn't meant his action to be a threat. Suddenly the good-looking ladies' man with laughing blue eyes and nicely crinkled hair seemed as deadly as a coiled rattler.

He raised a conciliatory hand. 'Easy now feller,' he protested. 'I meant no harm, restin' my hand on the pistol is just a habit.'

'It could be a fatal habit,' growled Pinter. Then a smile split his face; it was as if the sun had come out.

'Hell,' he grinned disarmingly. 'Guess I was more on edge than I figgered, what with these two a-growlin' at each other every goddamned day you've bin gone. Let's call it quits, huh?'

Tyler could hardly suppress a sigh of relief as Sam Pinter turned away and walked towards his pony. Out of the corner of his eye he saw the black man turn away also.

He stepped close to McBride. 'What the hell's gotten into you, Mac?' he muttered hoarsely. 'You know we need every man we've got if we're ever gonna git this herd rebranded and into Abilene. You'll have bags of time to kill the bastard once we've sold the herd; I'll even help you do it.'

'I don't need any help,' growled McBride. 'My Colt might not look very professional, Tyler, but I kin reach it awful fast if I have to.'

'Reckon Wes Calvin can also,' replied Tyler, a slight sneer in his voice. 'But for now, forget it, OK?'

'We'll see when the time comes; I don't mind waitin',' grunted McBride. 'You figgered the route yet?'

'Yep, we follow the river nice an' easy for the next three days or so, then we cut across to a place called Salt Fork. It'll mean four or five dry days so we take it easy an' let the herd drink all they want, they'll need it when the time comes.'

Tyler stomped over to the fire and poured himself a cup of coffee. He tilted his hat back on his head and found a place to sit on an old log.

The coffee was good and strong, it began to soothe his nerves a little as he stared out across the prairie, his mind turning over the recent events.

Was it Carl or Bart Simes who was pulling the strings? Or both, perhaps. He could write Calvin out; he'd been scared witless when he'd been shown the ranger badge, and Sam Pinter was representing an owner, and had a good solid riding background with the brand.

Virgil Calder now, he always seemed to be somewhere in the background. Those two Remingtons set in a cross-draw looked like they could be reached in a hurry, and while most cowpokes carried a Bowie or something similar, it was not often a man carried a second knife strapped to his leg at boot level and covered by his pants-leg.

His musings were interrupted as Calder picked up the coffee pot. 'We doin' anything about movin' the herd along today, boss?' he questioned.

'Yeah,' replied Tyler, eyeing the man closely, 'just keep 'em drifting along the bank up thataway. Take things easy, we'll have our hands full once we leave the river.'

Calder nodded, finished his coffee, threw the dregs into the fire and strolled towards his mount.

Tyler stared at the retreating man's back, still turning the disturbing possibilities over in his mind.

He was still wondering how he'd allowed himself to be persuaded by McBride into rustling the herd. He had to admit the idea was a clever one, almost foolproof, but it was too clever for a loud-mouth like McBride to have thought of it. The Simes brothers were quiet and taciturn; they didn't seem that intelligent, but a body could never be quite sure....

EIGHT

The Indians dragged the old man's body behind them for another half-mile before they stopped and cut the rope. When they rolled the body over there was nothing left of Ward Killick's face and chest except raw flesh.

The chieftain stared at Jeff; there was no expression on his face. 'He was old, it was his time to die,' he grunted.

'If the council decides that I should die, I challenge you to kill me as a warrior,' Jeff said bitterly. 'I would like to see your head on the end of my spear.'

From somewhere he found enough moisture in his mouth to spit. It landed on the chieftain's moccasin. '*Squaws* kill old men,' Jeff taunted through dry lips.

The Indian's face tightened in anger. 'If the council decides, I will fight you, white man, and your head will be on *my* lodge pole.'

The chief remounted and they continued the long trek to the Indian camp.

By the time they reached the encampment Jeff was barely able to stand, only raw animal determination kept him on his feet. His hands, strapped to the gun resting across his shoulders, were numb and his shoulders ached from the continuous weight.

The small group rode slowly past the wikiups

where women and children stopped to stare silently at the prisoner, but Jeff was beyond caring as he concentrated on planting one foot in front of the other.

The rope around his neck had caused a dull throbbing ache but the protection of his heavy coat collar, added to the thickness of his bandanna had cushioned him from the full brunt of the pain.

He felt the rope slacken as the pony ahead of him stopped. Jeff allowed himself a hoarse sigh of relief. With great effort he planted his feet apart and stood swaying like a tree in the wind.

The Indian dismounted and dragged him towards a circle of chieftains who had gathered around the open space in front of the chief's dwelling in response to the news that a prisoner was being brought into the camp. They halted again and Jeff braced himself against the swirling dizziness ... until the Indian kicked him behind the knee and he collapsed, the weight of the rifle across his back effectively stopping him from rising.

Through bleary eyes, red-rimmed and sore, he watched the stately figure of the chief step from his wikiup. The talk flashed backwards and forwards far too fast for Jeff to comprehend in his exhausted state. Then the chieftain was talking to him and had slowed his speech so that Jeff could understand.

'You hear me, white man?' asked the chief.

Jeff merely nodded, even that was painful.

'You will be taken to a place where you can rest and eat, then you will sleep for the passing of one moon, after that time you will go before the council. Do you understand me?'

Once again Jeff nodded.

There was a rapid exchange of words between the

minor chieftain who had captured him and the chief of the tribe. Jeff could tell that keeping and feeding the prisoner was not to his captor's liking. But the chief was angry also. From what little he could grasp, the chief did not agree with the mistreatment of the white prisoner.

A brave stepped forward and helped Jeff to his feet, supporting him as they walked together towards one of the dwellings.

'You will stay here,' the brave told him. 'I am to be your guard. If you try to leave I will kill you. A squaw will bring you food and water. You understand?'

Jeff nodded and thanked the brave in his own tongue as the Indian cut his arms free and removed the rifle.

The pain was so excruciating as Jeff lowered his arms to allow the brave to tie his hands together in front of him, that he had to bite his lips to stifle a betraying moan of agony.

'Food will come soon,' muttered the brave as he departed, leaving Jeff to endure the exquisite pain of stretching out on the dirt floor.

He hardly remembered eating, only the feel of the delicious water cooling and soothing his throat before he fell into a deep, energy-restoring sleep which lasted through the night and well into the following day when the squaw brought him more food.

Jeff thanked her for her kindness as she backed slowly out of the wikiup. He knew the squaw would not reply, but he thanked her anyway.

As the woman left, the Indian chief entered, standing with arms folded and feet apart staring wordlessly at Jeff, who slowly stood up and faced his captor.

The chief drew his knife and cut the bonds around his wrists.

'I have freed you, white man, but if you should try to escape the guards have orders to kill you.'

'I thank the chief of the Mescalero Apache for his kindness in allowing me time to recover before I face my trial,' Jeff said evenly.

'You realize that if the council decides you are to die, Running Deer has claimed his right to fight you to the death, white man? You will need all your strength; he is detemined to wipe the slur of "squaw" from your lips.'

'I will be ready,' responded Jeff. 'It is a poor warrior who would drag an old man to his death at the end of a rope. Kitchi Manito will guide my hand to avenge that shame.'

'You speak our tongue well, white man, and you know of the mighty spirit. I am ashamed for my people that the old man was dragged to death. Eat now and rest. The council will decide and you will be told of your fate when the moon is in the sky. I go now to the council.' The chief nodded and left.

Jeff ate well on the food provided, then he removed his heavy coat and empty holsters, and began to take the kinks out of his body with exercise.

Aching limbs protested at first but soon the old suppleness began to flow into his muscles. After two hours he rested and slept. When he awakened he resumed the exercise and by the time darkness had begun to close in Jeff knew he was as ready as he'd ever be.

Slipping the red bandanna from his throat he made sure that the thin strip of rawhide holding the sheath of the paper-thin knife was tucked as low as possible into his shirt so that it would not be visible in the light of the moon, then he retied the bandanna to cover the old rope-marks, scars over three years old from when a vindictive old man known as The Weasel had twice tried to hang him.

He had hardly finished before two braves entered, each carrying a tomahawk. They stood either side of Jeff and attempted to take hold of his arms.

'There is no need,' Jeff told them quietly. 'I am an honourable man, let the council decide.'

The braves released him and together they walked into the moonlit glade where the council members were sitting around the fire.

Running Deer was standing opposite the council and from the sullen glances the chieftain threw at him, Jeff realized that the council had been upbraiding him, probably over the death of Ward Killick.

Jeff waited in silence for the verdict as the chief rose to his feet.

'White man, Running Deer has called for you to be hanged like a dog, what say you to that?'

Jeff knew it was time to shock the chief and all the braves standing around waiting for the verdict. But more than anyone, he wanted to put the fear of superstition into Running Deer.

He slowly raised his hands to the red bandanna and peeled it away. 'I have already been hanged twice, yet I am not dead.' He touched the badly healed bullet scar on his forehead. 'See, I have also been shot by a white man's bullet, yet I have not entered the happy hunting grounds. I ask you to look, chief of the Mescalero Apache, and tell your people if this is so.'

A whisper of superstitious awe sounded from the braves as the chief stared closely before nodding solemnly. 'It is so,' he murmured, stepping quickly away.

Capitalizing upon the suspense Jeff strode boldly

up to Running Deer. 'See for yourself. *squaw*.' Jeff had no trouble putting venom and bitter contempt into his voice. 'Put your hand on the scars, place your finger into the hole made by the white man's bullet, feel them for yourself before you die.'

He pushed his face close and raised his head so that Running Deer could see the scars. 'Go on, *squaw*, touch the spot where Kitchi Manito tore the rope from my neck … twice! so that I should not die.'

There was another sigh of superstition from the braves as Running Deer reached forward to touch. But withdrew his hand as the fear gripped him.

Jeff slowly and deliberately slapped Running Deer's face. 'Where is your vow to fight me to the death, *squaw*?'

Running Deer forced himself to stare at his tormentor and slowly drew himself upright. 'I will fight you, white man. When the moon has gone and the sun first rises over the earth. Then we will fight to the death.'

Jeff, knowing that an Indian will rarely fight a one-to-one contest in the darkness because of his belief that if he should lose he would never find his way into the happy hunting grounds promised by Kitchi Manito, pressed home the advantage he had gained.

'The squaw is afraid he will lose, otherwise he would fight me now.'

He slapped the Indian's face a second time. 'Fight me *now*, squaw!' he snarled.

Driven into a frenzy at the continuous repeating of the insult by the white man, Running Deer snatched a knife from his belt and leapt towards his tormentor.

Even as Running Deer leapt, Jeff threw himself to one side. He hit the ground on his shoulder, rolled over in one movement and finished in a standing position leaving Running Deer poised near the fire facing the council and holding the bared knife in his hand.

'The squaw is willing to kill an unarmed man in the darkness but unwilling to fight as a warrior.' Jeff's voice was thick with the sneer. 'Is this the way of the Mescalero Apache?'

The council members were on their feet now and the chief made a signal to one of them. An elderly Indian stepped forward and handed Running Deer a tomahawk.

'A knife and a tomahawk are the only weapons to be used; the fight is to the death.' He spoke slowly so that Jeff could understand as he handed him his weapons. 'You understand, white man? Whether you win or lose will not change the decision of the council?'

Jeff gave a short nod of understanding as he accepted the knife and tomahawk.

He hardly had time to turn towards Running Deer before the Indian was upon him.

The tomahawk flashed in the firelight as it sliced towards his face. Only instant reflexes caused it to miss by the narrowest of margins as Jeff flicked his head to one side and heard the hiss of displaced air.

Almost in the same instant Running Deer's other hand struck upwards. Instinctively Jeff sucked in his stomach and turned away as the knife-point slit into his shirt cutting a shallow gash in the skin of his belly.

Having missed with both strikes, Running Deer kicked upwards, his moccasined foot landing squarely in Jeff's groin.

Screaming, sickening pain lanced through his stomach as he threw himself into a roll to get away from the Indian who seemed to be everywhere at once.

As he came out of the roll he just had time to see the Indian diving towards him, the tomahawk already beginning its lethal swing towards his head.

In sheer desperation Jeff threw up his arm in protection. His tomahawk glanced off the Indian's axe, deflecting it enough to throw Running Deer off balance, but the power of the Indian's blow whipped the tomahawk from his hand.

Ignoring the pain in his groin, Jeff dived into Running Deer while he was still off-balance. The Indian stumbled with the force of the charge, falling face down, arms spreadeagled with the white man on top of him. The Indian's hand holding the tomahawk was close and Jeff's knife chopped down. The hand spurted blood as the Indian lost three of his fingers.

Running Deer humped his back throwing Jeff over his head. Both men scrabbled to their feet. The Indian's hand was spurting blood, no longer able to hold the tomahawk. They charged towards each other the breath harsh in their throats as knife-point clashed with knife-point. The Indian forced the wounded hand into his opponent's face, attempting to blind him with its blood.

Jeff grabbed it with his free hand, forcing the remaining finger backwards until it snapped. An involuntary scream of agony was forced from Running Deer's lips and the hand holding the knife against Jeff's own, lost its pressure for a moment.

It was enough! Jeff released the bloodied hand and smashed his fist into the Indian's throat. The eyes widened as Running Deer tried to suck air into starved lungs. He dropped the knife in his agony and clutched his throat with both hands.

Slowly, like a felled oak he toppled backwards, mouth open wide. Unable to breathe he lay on his back attempting to suck air into his tortured throat.

Jeff stepped astride the fallen Indian, his body shaking like an aspen in the wind, the knife poised for the fatal thrust. He straightened and threw the knife aside.

'I give up my right to kill you,' panted Jeff hoarsely, as he too fought for breath. 'But you will no longer be known as Running Deer: it is a name for a brave warrior. From this day on you will be called Moaning Squaw. You will attend the dead, throw ashes over your body and moan for the departed. I give you your life, Moaning Squaw.'

Jeff turned slowly and staggered towards the council fire. 'I give thanks to the council of the Mescalero Apache and await the wisdom of your thoughts,' he husked.

There was a sudden disturbance behind him. Jeff turned and saw Running Deer on his feet. The Indian had snatched a lance from one of the braves and with the screech of a maddened animal, charged towards his enemy.

A rifle shot, almost beside Jeff, crowded out all other sounds. As if in slow motion he saw Running Deer stumble as blood spread across the Indian's face. The lance left his hand even as he fell.

Unable to move in the fraction of time left to him, Jeff watched in stunned fascination as the blade buried itself in the ground between his feet.

The member of the council who had fired the shot stepped up beside Jeff.

'My son, Running Deer, could not bear the disgrace,' he muttered, 'but I could not allow him to further disgrace my family by breaking the terms of the contest. By saving your life, white man, I shall decide upon your death.'

He turned to the council for their agreement; there were mutters and nods.

'This is fair,' agreed the chief. 'What have you decided?'

'That the white man may rest here and be fed until the moon has gone, and on the first rise of the sun he will be released. When the sun reaches the middle of the sky our people will hunt him to the death.'

'It will be so,' replied the chief. He nodded to the two braves who had brought Jeff from the wikiup. 'Take him back and guard him well. He will be released at the rising of the sun.'

The braves grabbed Jeff's arms, led him back to the wikiup and pushed him inside. 'Remember, white man, if you try to leave we will kill you,' growled one Indian.

'Why should I try to escape?' replied Jeff. 'Your council has said that I shall be released in the morning, unharmed, and I believe them.'

The Indian nodded. 'It is good that you believe them. We will leave you to eat and sleep.'

Once the braves had gone Jeff began to think of tomorrow; he would have six hours before the hunters began their search, not long for a man on foot. He knew the Indians would keep their word, because he had grown up in their company, but he was also a white man and Jeff had no intention of waiting until tomorrow to make his escape.

After he had eaten and the squaw had cleared away the remains of the meal, Jeff wrapped himself in the voluminous buffalo-skin blanket and lay down as if in sleep.

An hour passed on leaden feet before the guard

pushed aside the blanket covering the door and peered in. He was holding a burning branch high above his head so that he could see to check on the prisoner.

The brave seemed unsure and began to enter the wikiup so Jeff deliberately moved his feet, then turned on to his other side. Satisfied, the guard allowed the heavy blanket covering the doorway to drop back into place as he left.

Another hour passed and again the door covering was pulled aside.

Through lidded eyes Jeff watched as the man raised the flickering torch while he observed the muffled bundle in the middle of the floor. The brave studied the bundle for a short time before dropping the blanket as he also left, satisfied that the captive was still asleep.

The moment he had allowed the covering to fall into place Jeff slipped silently over to the doorway and peered out.

The two braves were settling down in front of the flickering fire and covering themselves with heavy robes to keep out the night's cold.

Moving like a ghost he collected everything in the wikiup that could be stuffed into his duster. Laying it on the ground, he wrapped the buffalo-skin blanket around it so that it looked as if he were still asleep.

Jeff knew that while a solitary mounted white man would stand little chance of survival in Indian country, a lone white man on foot would stand no chance at all, so he intended to become Indian.

He crept once again to the covered doorway and peered out at the braves. Everything now depended on how carefully they watched their prisoner. If they continued to check only from the doorway, the bundle on the floor would fool them, but if one of them decided to make a really close inspection they would be after him and he would stand no chance at all.

Jeff shrugged in the darkness. 'It's this or nothing fella,' he muttered as carefully he slit the bottom section in the wall of the wikiup at a point furthest away from the sleeping guards.

After a careful look around Jeff slid through the opening and pushed some of the sandy soil over the edges of the cut to hold it in place, then he belly-crawled towards the edge of the camp.

Jeff had contemplated sneaking up to the ponies with the intention of stealing one but he considered the risk too great.

The horses were usually guarded by at least one brave and two or three children; the slightest noise would start the half-wild ponies snorting and generally making a fuss which would quickly alert the guards. It would also make his intentions clear and, if possible, he wanted to just disappear giving the Indians no indication of where he was or what he was about.

Jeff wanted to be well away from the camp before the sun showed itself above the horizon, then he would use skills taught him by that wise old Indian, Eagle Eye.

Moving from rock to rock, avoiding any soft soil or sand he headed as swiftly as possible away from the Indian encampment. The weak light of the quarter moon gave him his direction and by the time the sun showed he had travelled several miles through the rocky territory.

What the fugitive needed now was a mounted Indian. They would be there, he knew that. Searchers would head out singly, in pairs or groups to hunt for him as soon as they became aware that he had escaped.

Jeff continued to move away from the camp for as long as he dared. The cool of the early morning was giving way to the heat of the day as he went to ground in a jumble of trees and boulders close to a barely discernible trail meandering through a small coulée.

His mouth was dry and his stomach was empty but he'd been in worse positions in the past. He cancelled these thoughts from his mind and concentrated on watching the trail below.

Nothing moved down there so Jeff decided to slip back into the trees to find something to eat. There were plenty of berries and other wild fruits in the woods and careful digging with his knife produced roots which were full of moisture.

He never moved far from his hiding-place because Jeff knew that no matter how well he tried to cover his tracks the Indians would quickly discover him.

For two days Jeff watched the narrow trail below him. On the first there was a flurry of activity as bands of Mescalero Apache rode backwards and forwards searching for him.

The second day the activity lessened as small bands began to search sections of the countryside looking for his spoor.

It was well past noon on the third day when Jeff watched a small band of Indians ride slowly through the coulée; there were four in all.

'Just three too many,' Jeff muttered.

He watched them intently as slowly they disappeared into a stand of timber ahead.

It was clear that the roving bands were closing in on him so, after a few moments' hesitation, he left his hiding-place and followed in their wake, always making sure that he left no sign of his passing. The boots were killing him by this time but he ignored everything that fell outside of his concentrated effort to remain unseen.

He was among the trees now, blessedly cool after the heat radiating off the rocks, but the softness underfoot warned him that he would have to be even more careful not to leave the slightest mark that would betray him.

Jeff had been moving forward for about an hour when he heard the snuffle of a horse somewhere behind him....

NINE

After easing the herd steadily along the banks of the Cimarron for three days, Matt Tyler ordered the men to begin bunching the cattle. They looked sleek and calm, ready at last for the waterless crossing.

Twice there had been sightings of Indians on the long ride some two miles away but they had not ventured any nearer.

Tyler told the men at supper that the herd would be turned and driven due north across the prairie at first light.

'We take 'em easy the first day so that they don't sweat out too much, but as we get out there the grass will become scarce so we pick up the pace a little on the second day, enough so's they're too tired to git edgy. Remember, boys, if they start runnin' there's no knowing how far they'll go and them war-whoops are just waitin' fer the chance to collect as many beeves as they can get. By day three they'll just be content to jog along, an' on day four they'll begin to smell the water ahead. They might start runnin' but keep 'em bunched an' they'll lead us to it.'

That night most of the men were allowed to stay in camp, and the watch over the herd was kept to a minimum.

It was near two o'clock when Wesley Calvin eased

his mount into the remuda and tethered it in the line.

He was about to make for the fire when he realized that two men were close by, talking in whispers.

The heavy walked-down grass had padded out the ground so that his approach would not have been heard above the sound of the shuffling hooves of the remuda.

Some sixth sense, probably developed in the war years, warned the man to silence, his dark blue uniform making him almost invisible in the darkness.

The conversation came to him in bits and pieces. One voice he recognized as Quincy McBride's. That man could never talk in a real whisper, Wes thought, as he tilted his head in an effort to recognize the other voice.

McBride was talking now, something about the herd. Then Wes heard him say quite clearly, 'Whatever else happens, mister, I'm gonna kill that god-damned Yankee.'

'Yeah OK,' the other voice replied, very softly and placatingly, 'just let's get the herd to market an' make our split.'

'Just the four of us, right?' That was McBride again.

Try as he might he could not place the other voice, it was too soft, barely above a whisper.

'Right!' agreed the voice. 'Now get out with the herd, Calvin will be in soon.'

Wes still could not place the voice, but McBride would be coming for his mount any time now so he slipped silently away, coming around towards the fire from a different angle, hoping to see who was out of their blankets.

He knew Calder was out with the herd because he'd been partnering him. Bart Simes was lolling on his blanket with a mug of coffee in his hand, Carl's bedroll was empty. He came towards the fire a few moments later, buttoning up his flies.

'That's better,' he grunted. 'I pour the coffee in one end an' it just flows out of the other.' He picked up an empty mug and filled it from the pot. 'Nice quiet night out there, Wes,' he continued. 'Could damn-near hear a man thinkin'.'

'Yeah,' agreed Wes. 'When are you on?'

'We take over from Quincy an' Sam so I guess we'd best get some shut-eye, Bart.'

As Carl was getting into his soogans Virgil Calder strolled in.

'You're late,' grunted Carl. 'You like it that much you kin have my share.'

'Oh yeah?' laughed Calder. 'Damned hoss was easin' along so gentle he near rocked me to sleep.' He picked up a mug, poured coffee and sat beside Wes. He noticed that the black man was staring at him.

'Somethin' eatin' you, Wes?'

'Um, no, just thinkin' is all, fella,' Wes grinned, ashamed of his thoughts. 'Any idea why we're leaving the main trail, Virgil?'

'Beats the hell outa me. Could be the trail boss has some better ideas. It's his job to guide, I just tag along.'

'I suppose,' replied Wes. 'This drifting along by the river sure has put the gloss back on their coats an' settled 'em down some, but I reckon there's somethin' kinda off centre about pulling off the trail like that. Don't you?'

'Like I said, Wes,' grunted Virgil as he prepared for sleep, 'he leads, I just follow orders an' earn my forty a month. G'night.'

Wes Calvin lay awake for quite a while pondering on what he had heard. Half-asleep he thought he heard a whispering between Calder and Carl Simes.

Instantly Wes was wide awake. He heard Virgil mutter, 'Keep it quiet, he might be awake.'

'You awake, Wes?'

That was Carl Simes's voice.

Wes didn't reply.

'Reckon he knows somethin'?' That was Carl again.

'No, don't think so. Now shut it an' git to sleep, lessen you wanna tell the whole damned world.'

That was the end of it and soon Wes could hear the steady quiet snoring of the two men before he too drifted off to sleep.

It seemed that he had hardly closed his eyes before the camp was being roused to the cobalt light of the false dawn and the appetizing smell of fresh-brewed coffee and bacon.

Within the hour, blankets had been rolled and strapped to the horses; there was no storage place for them now that they only had the one wagon.

Young Billy-Joe climbed aboard the replacement chuck wagon and kicked off the brake, heading due north away from the river as the men galloped out to the herd and began their cross-country drive.

Because of the shortage of men, Seth Calhoun had to ride drag and take care of his remuda as well, so each day one of the other riders had to join him at drag. Today, Wesley Calvin was detailed to ride with Calhoun.

The cattle seemed contented and moved easily along as they left the river behind and eased out on to the open prairie, so Wes and his partner had a fairly easy time. This close to the water the grass was fairly thick so the dust raised was minimal.

Wes was riding quietly along, musing over the conversation he had overheard when Seth Calhoun eased his pony up to him.

'Did you hear what I heard last night, Wes?' asked Seth diffidently.

'Depends on what you heard.'

'Last night. By the remuda line,' Seth amplified. 'Saw you standin' there in the dark while McBride was talkin' to his pal.'

'Who was the other one?' asked Wes.

'Dunno, couldn't make the voice; you?'

'No; what did you hear?'

'Same as you I reckon, it was about the herd. Sounded like a big steal to me, with only four in the final share-out. That how you heard it?'

'About like that,' agreed Wes.

'You was high on McBride's list. Sounded like a whole bag of grief for you, Wes.'

'Yeah wasn't it though. Still with only a four-way share-out at the end, 'pears to me that I ain't the only one who's gonna get the grief. Pity we can't place the other one.'

'I figger we should drift before we find ourselves in more trouble than we kin handle, Wes; I reckon we should pull out tonight. We're on the same watch; we could be three hours away before anyone wakes up to the fact that we're gone.'

The words came out in a rush once Seth had started and now he waited with bated breath for his partner's reaction.

'Where though, that's the rub,' replied Wes evenly. 'No use goin' ahead, an' if we cut back to the trail an' follow it to Abilene they could catch us easy by using all the spare remuda for mount changes.'

'I reckon we'd do better to go back the way we came. McBride wouldn't expect that, nor would Calder fer that matter. He's the clever one by my reckoning. I don't think they'd be able to spare anybody from the herd to go back. With us missing as well they'd be real short-handed.'

'I kin see you've bin givin' this an awful lot of thought, Seth, an' I reckon you've got the right of it,' replied Wes. 'Tonight then? They can't follow us in the dark anyway so we'd have a clear six hours before they can start. If we stay in the tracks back to the river they'll never be able to work out which way we've gone. Like you said, it's time to leave before it's too late.'

The two men drifted apart as Matt Tyler rode towards them shouting above the bellowing of the herd for the two men to keep well spread out in order to stop the cattle from bolting back to the water.

The man seemed to be in an aggressive mood so Wes and Seth merely nodded, and after a short while the trail boss fed steel to his pony and rode towards the front of the herd.

Wes glanced at the young remuda man and touched his stetson in acknowledgement of their agreement. Seth replied in kind as gradually they drifted further and further apart.

There was no more need for words, both men knew they had made a commitment to leave the trail herd when they took over the night shift....

The cattle were already missing the water by the time Wes and his riding partner collected their mounts and drifted slowly towards the herd for their night stint.

Calvin called softly to Calder as they passed him. 'All quiet Virgil?'

'Yep. A mite upset without the water, but they'll git over it. Tonight ain't too bad, tomorrow will be different.'

Seth grinned as Virgil disappeared in the darkness.

'He don't know how different,' Wes murmured.

TEN

Jeff faded silently into the undergrowth as the solitary Indian rode by, eyes intent on the tracks left by those other Indians somewhere ahead. He stayed as close as he dared without alerting the man who ambled on, still following the tracks.

Jeff froze, then slid slowly out of sight again as he heard the clump of hooves coming from the opposite direction.

It was the four Indians he had been following.

'Hoa,' shouted one of the group. 'Are you following us, Little Bear?'

'You have not yet found the white man?' asked the lone Indian.

'There is no sign of him, no sign at all. White men always leave sign so he cannot have come this far. We are returning to camp to see if others have found him. Ride to the village with us.'

'I will continue the search,' replied Little Bear. 'I would like to be called Mighty Hunter, and if I should find him I shall ask the council if I may have that honour.'

The four Indians laughed good-naturedly. 'We wish you good hunting, but no white man could have come this far on foot without leaving some sign.' He waved an airy hand. 'Search on little brother,' he called, as the four rode past.

Jeff closed his eyes and said a small prayer of thanks to his own particular spirit. Little Bear rode a good, healthy looking pony and he carried a bow, arrows and a knife. But best of all he was alone!

As soon as the four were out of sight, Jeff followed in the wake of the lone Indian who stopped after a short while and untied a small package from around his waist.

Jeff's mouth began to water as the Indian extracted a pemmican cake from the food pouch and began to munch with obvious relish.

He could almost taste the cured venison and the crushed berries that made up the cake.

'Don't eat 'em all fella,' Jeff muttered as he slid past, heading for a large jumble of boulders almost overhanging the trail ahead.

Once he was out of sight of the Indian he carefully eased around the rock and on to the trail, then he began treading into the soft soil at its base.

Having left some clear prints he back-tracked and climbed to the top of the boulder.

Drawing the knife from its sheath behind his neck, Jeff crouched on the top of the rock. From this vantage point he watched while his victim finished his meal.

Moments later, Little Bear closed his food pouch, tying it with a strip of rawhide, then kicked his mount into a slow walk.

Jeff concentrated on every movement as the Indian approached, his mind picking over his plan.

Had he left enough sign? Would the Indian do what Jeff expected him to do? Or would he suspect a trap and drive his mount away from that deadly boulder?

Jeff allowed the anxieties to flow over him without a change of expression or movement.

Everything would depend on how alert the Indian was and he was banking on the fact that, having eaten in a leisurely fashion with no trouble and now being comfortably satisfied, the Indian would become excited when he spotted the footprints below the boulder and be tempted over for a closer look.

Several agonizing minutes passed as the pony slowly ambled along but Jeff's face remained calm, his body poised, waiting for that vital moment when his plan would work or fail.

The horse was already past the boulder and Jeff was debating whether to attempt an almost impossible leap towards the mounted man, when the Indian suddenly tensed, reined in and eased his mount closer to the boulder, his eyes glued to the tracks.

Some instinct made Little Bear pause and glance upwards.

He tried to whirl his pony away and almost made it but was too late.

Jeff landed astride the pony, behind the Indian. The force of the landing almost made the horse collapse and both men slid off the pony's rump.

The man was as slippery as an eel, turning in Jeff's grasp, one hand reaching for the thong about his waist where the horn-handled knife dangled in a buffalo-hide sheath.

The knife was already half out when Little Bear's eyes opened wide in shock as Jeff's knife whipped across his throat and his life's blood spurted from the wound in a torrent. Even as he died, Little Bear managed to pull the knife all the way out of the sheath and make a weak thrust at his attacker.

Jeff felt the point of the knife press into his side,

but fell away as the Indian suddenly went limp in his arms.

'May Kitchi Manito welcome you to the happy hunting grounds, Little Bear,' Jeff murmured softly, as the limp form slumped to the ground.

But he knew this was no time for sentiment or regrets. Without bothering to glance at the Indian, Jeff set about calming the fractious pony and tethering it to a small sapling.

Picking up the dead man he draped him over the horse's back and led him away into the rocks.

Jeff travelled a long way into the rough country until he came to a brush-choked valley.

After tying the pony to a branch he lifted the Indian down and carried him into the brush. He was looking for a crevice deep enough to hide the body so that no one would find it. It took some time to find the right place but eventually he discovered a fissure between two huge boulders.

After removing all the clothes from the body he lowered it into the crevice then, stripping off his own clothing, he tied them into a small bundle together with the two empty holsters. He used his knife-torn shirt as a wrapper, with the sleeves tied together in a loop so that he could slip the cigar shaped bundle over his shoulder and leave both hands free.

He quickly donned the breech clout and shirt, tied the Indian's knife around his waist and slipped on the moccasins. They were on the big side but by pulling in the gut-strings it tightened the moccasins enough to keep them in place. They were a welcome relief to the boots which he dumped into the crevice.

Dressed as an Indian the roving bands would not give him a second glance. They would be looking for a white man, afoot, and probably in a distressed condition.

Jeff knew that the juice of certain berries would soon change the colour of his skin, and the two feathers that had so recently adorned the head of Little Bear would add to the illusion, so that even close-up it would be difficult to spot him as a white man, except for his eyes of course, but Jeff didn't intend to let *anyone* get that close.

He carefully rolled some rocks and boulders into the crevice so that not even predators would be able to get at the body. The last thing he wanted was for the Indians to be alerted by carrion birds in the sky.

Satisfied, he obliterated all trace of his passing and rode away slowly back to where he had ambushed Little Bear, munching contentedly on a pemmican cake as he rode.

When Jeff arrived back at the boulder he cautiously searched the area for other intruders before wiping out his booted footprints.

He did not bother with the new tracks. Anyone coming upon them would see the sign of an unshod pony and moccasin prints, so they would assume that an Indian had made them.

It could be several days or even weeks before the Indians would consider Little Bear. His friends would tell of his determination to continue the hunt for the glory of being renamed, Mighty Hunter, and every Indian in the camp would understand Little Bear's need for such an honour.

Jeff was grateful to the Indian for providing so many things, the clothes he wore, the pony, a knife, bow and arrows and pemmican too.

He smiled grimly; maybe Little Bear hadn't wanted to part with all those things but this was tough country.

Jeff left the trail and cut into the forest to look for the berries he intended to use to stain his skin the dark mahogany colour that would allow him to blend with the people looking for him. He was as much at home here as any Indian and now his chances of survival were very good indeed.

At last he could begin to consider what had happened to the cattle and why he and Ward Killick had been left behind at the mercy of the Indians. Jeff stared into the darkness of the night as he lay beside his flickering camp-fire and searched for reasons.

Why had Wesley Calvin suddenly become so unfriendly? Was it all because of the ranger's badge he had carried? Why was the trail boss determined to leave him and Ward behind? If it was only because of the badge, why leave Ward?

Jeff could dimly remember Matt Tyler seeming to be taking orders from Quincy McBride. Why?

The questions seemed to tumble over each other, but there were no answers. He shrugged resignedly as he carefully buried the fire in soil to smother it.

One thing was sure, he thought, as he lay upon the warm ground where the fire had been; snugly wrapped in the folds of the horse blanket: the men with the herd all expected him to be dead by this time. That was a mistake and sooner or later there would be a reckoning.

In the meantime he'd use every trick he knew to get through the Indian Territory. There was some catching up to do. The trail herd should be well up towards the Kansas border by this time.

Once they were within a few miles of Abilene, Matt Tyler would probably hold the cattle on good grazing for a week or two so that they could regain the weight loss of the drive. Then he would ease them slowly into the town ready for the stock yards.

Jeff wanted to be there when the cattle were sold. He represented two-thirds of the herd now that Ward Killick was dead.

His mind was still attempting to solve the problem when sleep claimed him.

ELEVEN

Over the next two weeks Jeff kept the great brown swathe of the herd's tracks in sight but stayed well away from them.

Several times he saw small bands of Indians crossing and recrossing the tracks but by keeping to the foothills he managed to remain unseen.

Jeff not only looked like an Indian but he also thought and acted like one, and livng off the land came as second nature to him.

He could see by the great curve in the cattle trail ahead that it would be leading towards a river crossing, otherwise there would be no need to change direction on these lands of great undulating prairie.

Jeff eased out of the foothills towards the cattle trail, every nerve tingling, expecting at any moment to hear the high 'yip yip' call of Indians chasing him.

Most of the Indian Territory was unknown to whites but there was always some knowledge, carried by plainsmen and the like, who had braved these dangerous lands in the past. As far as Jeff could recall he was moving into Kiowa territory now so he had to be doubly cautious.

Surrounded as they were by three different tribes the Kiowas would react savagely to anyone found on their hunting grounds. Red or white.

Jeff was riding slowly towards a rise in the land ahead when he heard a flurry of gunshots, and faintly on the slight breeze he heard the high-pitched call of Indians.

He dismounted and hurried towards the lip of the rise, leading his mount behind him by the hackamore in case he needed it in a hurry.

Just before he reached the drop-off he tethered the pony to an outcrop of rock and began a crouching run up to the rim. Jeff heard the distinct boom of a Colt handgun. Indians rarely used pistols so it had to be white people, he decided, as he threw himself flat and peered over the edge.

The reason for the curve in the cattle trail was now obvious: Jeff was lying on a ridge of rock with a sheer drop below of some fifty feet into a river, the trail looping around to where the ground sloped down gradually towards the river crossing.

He could see two men in standard range gear crouching directly below him.

They had obviously been driven across the river into the shelter of the rocks by the Indians on the opposite bank who were keeping out of pistol range and firing arrows high into the air, allowing them to drop among the rocks where the cowboys were hiding.

The two men had given good account of themselves; Jeff could see three Indians lying in the dust close to the riverbank but the remaining half-dozen were playing a waiting game, showing themselves for a brief moment, just long enough to tempt the trapped men into wasting another bullet.

It was only a matter of time. Either the two men would be foxed into using all their bullets or perhaps the Indians had already sent one of their number to fetch help.

The answer was soon forthcoming. On a distant hill, way behind the Indians, a column of smoke lifted into the still air. A message was being sent so the fate of the men below was sealed.

Jeff watched the horizon for the return signal, and after a short wait an answering column of smoke lifted in the distance.

The Indians below had been watching also. They yipped their excitement and sent a further shower of arrows into the air.

Jeff was concentrating on their chatter to try to gain some idea of their plans.

He heard some mention of another brave who had been sent....

His concentration was abruptly interrupted by the swish of displaced air. It told Jeff where the brave had been sent!

He threw himself to one side and a tomahawk buried itself in the grass beside him. The stink of buffalo fat almost smothered him as the Indian landed across his body.

In desperation Jeff wrapped his arms around the brave but the fat smeared on the Indian's body made it impossible to hold him as they rolled over and over.

The brave drove a knee towards Jeff's groin but he managed to deflect it with his thigh as he jabbed two straight fingers towards the Indian's eyes.

The man saw it coming and his teeth locked down upon Jeff's fingers.

The brave must have thought he had Jeff at his mercy as he sat astride him and gripped the wrist with both hands. He opened his mouth to get a better grip with his teeth.

Jeff's other hand stabbed at the brave's eyes, this time with more success. The Indian grunted his pain as the two fingers jabbed into his eyelids and Jeff was able to throw him sideways so that the Indian was now on the ground but with his legs still wrapped around Jeff's lower body.

Temporarily blinded, the brave's hands scrabbled for purchase. His hand came into contact with the tomahawk with its blade half-buried in the ground.

He snatched out the weapon and swung it towards his adversary, but Jeff managed to avoid it. His hand flicked to the back of his neck. The thin blade slipped into his hand and Jeff felt the skin on the brave's neck give as the blade slid home. He dragged it sideways and the Indian went limp as a fountain of blood spurted from the ruptured artery.

Jeff lay there for a few moments, the stink of buffalo fat mixed with the iron-smell of blood wafting over him as he sucked air into his lungs. Then he threw himself off the dead man, eyes searching urgently for other dangers.

He could see no one else on the slope. Jeff wiped his knife on the dead man's shirt and slipped it into its sheath as he tried to understand why the Indians below had sent only one brave to make the attack from above.

He saw the indistinct shape of a long gun in the grass where the Indian had dropped it before attacking him.

After another quick scan of the area, Jeff made a crouching run towards it.

Now he knew why the Indians had sent only one man. One rifle fired over the lip would quickly put the two men below in real trouble.

The gun was an old Sharps single shot buffalo gun its hexagonal barrel rusted with neglect. There was a pouch of bullets tied to the long-looped trigger guard.

Jeff pulled open the breech-gate and squinted down

the barrel. It was dusty and gritted. He opened the pouch and the heavy calibre cartridges too, felt furry with dirt and dried grease. He frowned as he dropped one into the loading gate and heard the harsh rasp as he closed it.

Firing the gun in its present state would probably be more dangerous to himself than to the Indians he thought dourly, as he made his crouching run back up the slope. If he didn't do something soon though, the two white men down there would be in big trouble when the rest of the Indians arrived in response to the smoke signal.

Peering cautiously over the rim, Jeff saw that the Indians were still tempting the two men below into wasting cartridges.

Both were using pistols, leading him to the conclusion that either they did not have long guns or they were out of ammunition for them.

One Indian, obviously a minor chieftain, was becoming increasingly daring. Aware that he was out of range he would ride his horse into the clearing and pirouette contemptuously while waving his coup stick before riding back into cover.

'Here goes nothin',' muttered Jeff from his prostrate position, as he drew a bead on the space between the rocks. 'Show yourself again, mister, an' let's see what this old blunderbuss can do.'

Jeff hated the thought of what would happen when he fired the gun, but as the Indian once again galloped boldly forward Jeff slowed his breathing, then held it for a second before depressing the trigger.

The heavy buffalo gun roared, belching a blinding cloud of smoke. The Indian was lifted from his pony as if by a giant hand and thrown several feet away.

The butt of the rifle slammed into Jeff's shoulder like a charging buffalo, almost knocking him back from the ridge and forcing a yell of pain from him. His shoulder felt numb but he knew that he had to go on.

He flipped open the loading gate.

Jeff hoped that the shot had cleared most of the rubbish out of the barrel but as a safety measure he spat on the next cartridge and spread the spittle along its length before dropping it into the slot and closing the gate. He figured any kind of lubricant was better than nothing.

Jeff peered over the rim. The Indians had moved further back out of range of the normal carbine; they had no conception of the distance a Sharps buffalo gun could fire.

The Indians were grouped together in the open staring in obvious consternation at the ridge. Jeff aimed at another who seemed to be in charge, judging by his waving and shouting. The gun roared again. The Indian exploded from the group and crashed back into the rocks.

The punch of the recoil was not quite so bad this time. Jeff flipped open the loading gate and slid another spit-loaded cartridge into the breech. He slammed it shut and aimed in the general direction of the madly gesticulating Indians.

By sheer luck the bullet smacked into a boulder between the bunch: splinters of rock were flying in all directions, the Indians jumping around as if they were being attacked by a swarm of hornets.

Almost on reflex Jeff flicked open the gate again, the cartridge was slotted in and a fourth shot was on its way. This was too much for the remaining four who began to dodge and run further away from such accurate shooting.

Encouraged by the help from the rim, the two men below gave easily recognized cowboy yells as they mounted their horses and drove them into the water, firing their pistols in defiance as they came.

Jeff sent two more shots after the retreating Indians before allowing himself to relax.

Rubbing his sore shoulder he watched the two men below turn their mounts into the river crossing and ride around the long curve towards his position.

Jeff grinned as he saw them riding up the slope. They were in for a shock when they saw what they would think was a full-blood Indian waiting for them.

The easy grin slowly died as he recognized the two riders. He flipped open the loading gate, another cartridge slid home, the gate closed with a final-sounding snap....

TWELVE

Wesley Calvin and Seth Calhoun rode slowly around the herd in opposite directions. It took them nearly half an hour to meet up having made a full circle.

'Looks as if they're settlin' down OK,' murmured Wes.

'Yup. If we're gonna go, I reckon now would be the time,' grunted his partner. 'We'll have to take a chance an' hope they stay quiet.'

'If they run let's hope they don't run back towards the river; I don't want to look over my shoulder an' see that lot piling up behind us,' replied Wes.

'You always this cheerful?'

'Sometimes I'm even happier.'

'Glad you told me,' muttered Seth. 'Do we leave now or do you want to cheer me up some more?'

By mutual consent they edged away from the herd keeping their mounts at a slow walking pace for a mile or so before easing them into a lope.

The sky was as black as pitch, the moon was covered by lowering clouds and the air was beginning to tingle with static electricity.

'Looks like a storm coming up,' shouted Seth above the noise of the horses' hooves.

'Yeah, hope nobody notices what's happening before it breaks, otherwise Tyler might send somebody after us.'

'Somebody? Like who?'

'Like Calder maybe, or Quincy McBride,' replied Wes. 'Either way we've got no choice now but to go.'

The two men leaned further forward in their saddles and lifted their broncs to a gallop as a fitful moon broke through the cloud lending its weak light to warn them of any pitfalls.

Lightning flitted across the sky brightening the prairie for a moment, only to leave the landscape darker than before, but the threatened storm did not materialize and the horses continued to put space between the two fleeing men and the trail herd.

By dawn they had crossed the Cimarron and were on the Chisholm Trail heading for the North Canadian.

All they had with them were their water bottles. It had been impossible to obtain any food from the chuck wagon; young Billy-Joe took his new job as cook very seriously, so they had no chance of stealing anything.

Sun-up saw the two men riding back along the dark brown trail at a lope, slowing to a fast walk as the sun began to warm the earth.

'Reckon we should get away from the trail a bit an' look for some game,' Wes said. 'Might be a good idea to drop back into the foothills yonder. I don't think Tyler will send anybody after us now.'

'Won't git much out here in the open,' agreed Seth, as with one accord they eased towards foothills where, in the distance, timbered slopes promised both protection and game.

The two men spent a week easing their way through the timber, always keeping the dark brown of the Chisholm Trail in sight, and heading back towards Texas.

They fed off any game that came to their crude snares, balancing their diet with fruit and berries. Water was not a real problem as there were many small freshets among the trees, but they both longed for a good cup of arbuckle.

'Good drop of water,' grunted Wes as he threw away the dregs.

'Yeah but it don't nohow beat a good cup of coffee,' replied his companion grumpily.

'Be grateful fer the water,' answered Wes. 'I remember during the war...'

'Oh God!' groaned Seth Calhoun, in mock disgust. 'You ain't gonna start about the war agin are you? To hear you tell it you won the damned war all on your ownsome.'

'Almost did,' came the complacent reply. ''Course there *were* a couple of other fellas there at the time. Did I ever tell you...'

'Probably,' interrupted Seth. Then he stiffened in alarm. 'Somethin' movin' back in there, Wes,' he muttered, as he slowly picked up his carbine and began to ease himself from his sitting position.

At the first sign of Seth's change from easy banter to tenseness, Wes also picked up his rifle and began to get to his feet.

'Gently does it, pardner,' he muttered between clenched teeth. 'Ease slowly towards the tree behind you.'

Two arrows flitted from between the trees passing close to Seth.

'Slowly my ass!' shouted the young wrangler as he dived towards the tree for protection, while Wes rolled desperately towards a second tree as an arrow tugged at his jacket before he could make cover.

Seth dropped behind his tree and sprayed the

brush with bullets as fast as he could jack each cartridge into the firing chamber. Then Wes also began to shoot until his rifle clicked on empty.

There was no reply from the trees as the two men reloaded. Seth lifted the gun to his shoulder, ready to start firing again.

'Leave it!' shouted Wes. 'They ain't out there now, they're long gone an' all that shootin' is gonna draw every Indian in the Territory down on our backs. Let's grab the broncs an' git out of here *pronto*.'

The two men cautiously eased through the scrub and collected their horses; they did not even try to pick up the sundry items they had left in the tiny clearing.

Thankful that their horses were still where they had left them, they climbed aboard and moved off as quickly and as quietly as they could.

They had put a good two miles behind them and were beginning to breathe easier again when more arrows came flitting through the trees.

With one accord they fed steel to their mounts and began a crazy zig-zagging dash. Branches seemed determined to sweep them from their saddles as they crashed along the narrow game trail in an attempt to out-run the Indians. But they both knew they were wasting their time.

The Indians would be on foot, moving faster and much quieter than the two horsemen, while one or two of their comrades would be following behind, leading their mounts.

'Let's git into the open if we can,' shouted Wes as they charged along. 'Maybe we kin find some rocks or somethin'.'

Seth did not reply. He was a young man and the fear of an early death was in his eyes as they sped into a coulée, dismounting on the run as arrows searched for them.

Neither man released the reins as they dragged the horses into shelter; they knew that afoot they would stand no chance of survival.

They had dragged long guns from their saddle-boots as they dismounted. Now they rolled into the protection of the boulders and did a rapid reload.

Wes started cursing. 'How are you off for ammunition, Seth?' he asked anxiously.

'Just what's in the magazine,' came the terse reply. 'You?'

'Same. Rest is for the handgun so take it easy, OK?'

But it was as if the Indians knew. Flitting shadows tempted the two men into taking shot after wasted shot, until the long guns were empty.

'That's it,' snarled Calvin as he tugged two extra sixguns from under his shirt and placed them on the rocks beside him.

Seth stared at the two guns accusingly. 'Where did you get them, Wes?'

'They're Mason's.'

'You *stole* 'em? Left him out there with *no guns*? Man, you sure must hate the guy...'

'He was a ranger,' interrupted Wes defensively. 'He was after my hide. What was I supposed to do? Let him take me in for the reward? I could have shot him. McBride even offered me these guns to do it, but I didn't, did I?'

Seth had instinctively moved away from Wes. 'With no guns? In Indian territory?' The young man's voice carried a sneer. 'Maybe it woulda bin kinder to have shot the *hombre*, fella.'

A shower of arrows fell into the rocks around them, cutting off the conversation and both men started pumping bullets at shadows again.

'We've got to take a chance an' ride out of here fast,' snapped Wes. 'We'll soon be out of cartridges at this rate.'

'Let's do it,' replied his companion, as he jumped to his feet and slapped his mount, sending the startled animal leaping forward.

Seth hit the saddle on the run and leaning far over, spurred the horse into a mad gallop.

Wes was only seconds behind as arrows showered around them.

Gut instinct made Seth drive the animal directly towards the bushes where the Indians were hiding, firing his pistol along his mount's neck as he rode.

Wes was beside him now, firing as fast as he could trip the hammer.

There was a mad scrambling ahead as their enemies scurried to get out of the way of the charging horses.

Suddenly they were through! Out on the open plains, riding like demons, they made no attempt to reload as they leaned over their horses' necks, coaxing every ounce of speed from the mustangs.

The yipping, yelling Indians burst from the trees a few moments later. Superb horsemen, riding as only they knew how, firing the occasional arrow in the hope of a lucky hit but still wary of the white men's guns.

Slowly the Indians began to overhaul the two men as they sped along the great curve in the Chisholm Trail.

Wes realized that by following the curve they were taking the longest route to the small tributary river ahead and that their pursuers, by cutting across it, were rapidly closing the distance.

The two men also began to cut the curve but they could hear the pound of hooves behind them now and arrows began to drop all around them.

Directly ahead the river curved into a cliff-face. It was almost sheer for about fifty feet. Climbing it, either on horseback or afoot, was out of the question yet they could not afford the time to ride around to the crossing.

A glance to their left told them that the Indians had already cut off that escape route.

Wes powered into the river closely followed by Seth. As they reached the opposite side they dismounted on the run, driving their horses into a small cut-off in the rocks before turning and dropping to one knee, ready for a last desperate stand. Fumbling fingers hastily rammed fresh cartridges into sixguns.

The Indians, made bold by the lack of gunfire, threw themselves from their ponies and charged towards the water.

Guns loaded at last, the two men fired as fast as they were able. One. Two. Three Indians fell under the fusillade before they realized that the two white men were still able to fight back. The remaining six ran back towards the rocky section to the right of the trail while Wes and Seth dropped into their own cover.

'Only a matter of time, pardner,' muttered Wes, as he punched fresh shells into the twin Colts. 'Looks like I've dragged you down with me.'

'We ain't dead yet,' growled Seth. 'An' we'll damn-well take some of the bastards with us before we go.'

Wes pointed to an Indian racing towards the river crossing up ahead. He was carrying an old Sharps buffalo gun.

'He's gonna be up there somewhere, son. Ain't no way we-all is gonna be able to keep out of *his* sight. No, looks like the end of the line,' Wes finished dispiritedly.

'We'll *still* take some of 'em with us,' snarled Calhoun. 'I ain't givin' in that easy.' He fired two shots in defiance at one of the Indians but they were well out of range.

'Pity we left our long guns back there in the trees,' he muttered.

'Didn't have any shells fer 'em anyway,' grumbled Wes. 'We'd best keep an eye up there,' he continued. 'That war-whoop sure is takin' his time.'

On the heels of his comment the heavy boom of the Sharps sounded from above. Both men instinctively ducked.

They watched in amazement as a young chieftain who had been tempting them to waste ammunition was suddenly catapulated from his mount.

'That Indian up there must be one lousy shot,' muttered Wes disbelievingly. 'Glad he's on their side.'

A second shot picked up another minor chieftain and slapped him against the rocks.

'Goddammit, Wes. We got help up there!' shouted Seth.

They watched spellbound as two more shots followed, and suddenly the Indians were running back to more secure shelter.

'Let's go!' shouted Wes as he tucked the twin sixguns into his belt, dragged his pony out of the cut-back and threw himself into the saddle.

With his pardner close behind him they drove their mounts into the river yelling their defiance. Seth fired some ineffectual shots into the air as they dashed to the crossing and up around the ridge towards their unknown helper....

THIRTEEN

Jeff could feel the blood burning hot as he watched Wesley Calvin and Seth Calhoun ride up the slope.

He had no grudge against the young wrangler but Calvin had been there while he was down. McBride had asked the black man if he'd wanted to shoot him while he had lain almost unconscious in the mud.

As they approached, Jeff lifted his body out of the concealing grass, elbows balancing him as he aimed the old Sharps at Calvin.

Both men drew their mounts to a halt. Jeff heard Calhoun mutter disbelievingly, 'It's a goddamned Apache Indian, Wes. What are we gonna do?'

'He saved our lives back there so he can't be all bad,' replied Wes. 'You speak Apache?'

'Ain't no call for you to speak Apache, Calvin,' growled Jeff, as he centred the gun on the big man's chest and came up on one knee. The click of the heavy gun sounded loud in the stillness.

'That ain't *you*, Mason, is it?' Wesley Calvin was poised on his mount, almost like an animal sensing a predator and ready to bolt at a second's notice. But the hand poised above his sixgun said he wasn't about to go down without a fight.

'You make one move towards that gun an' it's the last thing you ever do, Calvin,' Jeff told him coldly.

'An' don't you git any ideas either, Seth. I ain't got a damned thing against you yet so let's keep it that way, huh?'

Calhoun slowly raised his hands to shoulder height. 'It's twixt you an' him, Mason. I didn't know anythin' until it was too late. Couldn't have done anythin' if I had, but I ain't about to help a man who left you unarmed in Indian country so I'll ride back a'ways if that's OK by you.'

'Be a good idea, feller,' answered Jeff evenly.

'Just one thing though,' added Calhoun as he made to turn his mount. 'Figger it would pay you to listen to his story before y-all blow his head off.'

'Nice to have friends!' growled Calvin, as Calhoun rode slowly out of pistol range, up towards the ridge.

'You got somethin' to say, mister, best git it said.' Jeff's voice sounded like cold water running over ice.

'Like you said, Mason. McBride asked me if I wanted to shoot you. Yes?'

'Somethin' like that.' The big Sharps didn't waver.

'You're still alive, mister, so why didn't I?' Wesley Calvin's tone was uncompromising.

'You're tellin' the story so git to it.'

'A lawman is after my hide for the bounty. I saw your badge an' I wasn't about to let you take me in. Still ain't fer that matter.'

The hand was still poised above the sixgun like a rattler waiting to strike. 'You wanna take me? Then take me fair, Mason. I'm carryin' your Colts … if you feel like usin' 'em.'

In spite of himself Jeff allowed the Sharps to sag a little. He'd never expected to see his guns again, guns that had once belonged to his father.

'I *ain't* a damned ranger, mister. I was carryin' the badge for a friend. So why the hell should I be huntin' you? I didn't even know you until you joined the trail herd.'

The big man's hand also eased away from his gun. 'I know someone's after me, was told it was you.'

'Who told you?'

'McBride. He found the badge in your pocket...'

'Um. I don't wanna hurry you, fellers,' interrupted Seth Calhoun, 'but there's another bunch of war-whoops down there by the river, so d'you think we could carry on this conversation some place else? I like my hair just the way it is ... if you get my drift.'

Jeff slowly allowed the gun to sag even more as he eased the hammer forward and climbed to his feet.

'Let's ride,' he growled. 'We'll settle all this later.'

He flipped himself aboard the Indian pony and kneed it towards the timbered hills.

'Follow me,' he grunted as he rode past the two men. 'An' try not to leave too wide a trail for 'em to follow, remember you're ridin' shod horses.'

Jeff set off at a gallop until he reached the protection of the foothills. Only when the tree-clad slopes gave him cover did he ease the pace to a fast trot and the other two pulled alongside.

'Figgered you was dead,' remarked Seth. 'You look pure Indian, even close-up.'

A wintry smile washed across young Mason's face. 'Guess you ain't the only one who thought I was dead, Seth. I ain't that easy to get rid of as Tyler an' McBride is gonna find out.'

'You goin' after 'em?' Seth asked incredulously.

'You think I'm gonna let 'em get away with that herd?'

'We've got to git outa this fix first,' interjected Wesley Calvin. 'Them Indians will be comin' close behind unless I miss my guess.'

'They might come,' conceded Mason, 'but they'll do it slow. We're back in Mescalero territory now. I figger the river is a kinda borderline. The Kiowas won't be lookin' to take on the Apache just to capture a couple of whites.'

'Nice to know we ain't gonna get bored,' grunted Wes, 'A change of scenery is nice, but one Indian is as bad as the next in my book.'

'Worse,' replied Jeff. 'The Mescalero caught me an' Ward Killick. Ward died; I escaped. I guess that could give 'em an edge over the Kiowas.'

'Sounds reasonable,' answered Calhoun.

'Don't worry, we won't be in their territory long. We're making a long curve; by tomorrow we'll be back at the river, then we'll cut for the Chisholm Trail again. There's a small cave up ahead, we'll stay there until first light.'

'How come you know of this here cave?' asked Seth.

'Used it a few nights ago; should be safe enough there as long as one of us keeps watch.'

The evening shadows were closing in by the time Jeff led them into a brush-choked canyon and dismounted in front of what appeared to be an unbroken slab of the canyon wall.

The others followed his lead and walked their ponies through the trees. The slab gave a false impression of solidity.

Behind it was a slit just wide enough for a horse to pass through into a cave.

From the rear there came the sound of dripping water, and a few moments later they were at the edge of a large pool. The horses pushed forward eagerly and began to drink.

'Some place you've got here,' grunted Wes. 'All the comforts of home.'

'You can bet the Mescaleros know it's here but I'll go back and wipe out our trail anyway,' replied Jeff, as he slid the cigar-shaped bundle from his shoulder. 'No point in makin' it easy for 'em. While I'm gone I'd like you to think about that ranger business, Wes. I'm willing to call it quits, an' if that suits you, I'd be obliged to see my Colts resting on that bundle when I get back.'

He passed the buffalo gun and the small pouch of ammunition to Seth Calhoun. 'One of you had better keep watch at the entrance 'til I get back but don't shoot unless you have to, OK?'

Without waiting for a reply Jeff slipped out of the cave and was gone.

'The fella moves like a cat,' grunted Seth, as he hefted the Sharps. 'Don't know why he gave me this, I kin manage with my sixgun.'

'Take it anyway, but don't forget, there's still one in the breech an' them old guns is awful light on the trigger,' warned Wes. 'You take first watch, I'll take over later, OK?'

It was full dark and Wesley Calvin was standing beside Seth having a muttered conversation before taking over the watch when Jeff appeared beside them, a silent dark shadow in the night.

'Jesus H. Christ! Where the hell did you spring from?' ejaculated Seth.

'If you want to keep your hair on, you'd do well to keep your mouth closed, your eyes open an' your ears a-listening,' Jeff grunted, as he slid silently into the cave followed by his two companions. 'There's no one about as far as I can tell so we'd best get some sleep while we can. We'll take two hours watch apiece.'

There were grunts of agreement from the other two and Wes volunteered to take the first watch with

Jeff taking the middle, while Seth would take the final one.

The night passed without trouble and the men were up, ready to ride at first light.

'No supper an' no breakfast sure gets a man outa his soogans kinda smart in the mornings,' grunted Wes.

'Saves a lot of time,' agreed Jeff, as he glanced at his cigar-shaped bundle and saw the two Colts lying on the top of it.

'Guess that means we've sorted our problems, huh, Wes?'

'Yeah; McBride kinda lit a fire under me for a spell with his tale of bounty hunters. Sure am sorry about that, Mason.'

'Jeff sounds about right, fella.'

The reply brought a remembering smile to Calvin's face as he held out a hand and Jeff gripped it for a moment.

'You two gonna kiss an' make up all day?' grunted Seth as he pretended to fuss around the horses. 'Or is one of us gonna scout around to see if there's any war-whoops out there?'

'I'll go an' take a look-see,' replied Jeff self-consciously as he picked up the six-guns, tucked them into the top of his breech clout and hooked his bundle over his shoulder.

'Sure appreciate you takin' care of 'em for me, Wes,' he murmured as he slipped out of the cave.

He returned a short while later, entering as silently as he had left.

'Looks as if we've got a clear field. Reckon the Kiowas stayed the other side of the river, and the Apache has already searched all this section once when they were lookin' for me. I reckon we should head towards the river but keep in the timber. With any luck we should be able to strike the Chisholm Trail where it meets the Cimarron in about a week or so.'

'Still headin' towards Abilene then?' asked Wes.

'Where else?'

'We figgered Texas,' replied Seth diffidently.

'Your choice.' Jeff was already collecting his pony and guiding it towards the opening. 'See you around.'

'Look over your shoulder, I'll be there,' grunted Calvin. 'Those *hombres* figgered to shoot me; I don't cotton to that at all.'

'Guess we're all going the same way then,' grinned Calhoun. 'I ain't goin' all the way to Texas on my own, 'sides, I'm afraid of the dark.'

'Yeah, that figgers,' grunted Wes as they all single-filed out of the cave and pushed their horses into a canter.

FOURTEEN

By using all his skill, Jeff led his two companions through the foothills without trouble. He had changed back into his own clothes and the two Colts were once again snug in their holsters. He had not discarded the bow and arrows however, and during the past week he had proved that in Indian country, the weapon had no equal in providing game without alerting the enemy.

The three men were at the junction where the Cimarron crossed the Chisholm Trail. It was easy to see where the cattle had turned to follow the river.

'We drifted the cattle along the riverbank fer three days before turning off on to the prairie. From what I heard when Matt Tyler was dishing out the orders, Salt Fork, was the place they were headin' for,' replied Wes, in answer to Jeff's question, as he pushed the stopper into his full water canteen and swung back into the saddle.

'They were sleek, fat and sassy by the time we started the crossing. That's when Seth an' me decided to leave 'em to it. Matt Tyler reckoned it would take five days to make Salt Fork.'

Jeff stared at the point where the herd had followed the river, seeing in his mind's eye the herd drifting steadily along, estimating times and distance

114

as dusk slowly closed in.

'Seems like they're adding around three weeks to the trip one way and another,' he mused. 'Wonder if that's where they're gonna blot the brands?'

'Makes sense,' opined Seth, as he also finished filling his canteen and stomped up the river bank. 'Give the new brands plenty of time to scud out so's they won't be noticed. Wouldn't do to drive into Abilene with raw brands now, would it?' he grunted as he swung into his saddle.

'Do we ride for the herd, or Abilene?' queried Wes.

'Abilene,' replied Jeff without hesitation. 'We're almost out of ammunition an' if they're gonna rebrand 'em we'll have plenty of time to get there and wait. They can't do all that, short-handed as they are, in less than five or six weeks. From here on we're ahead of 'em.'

'You still set on puttin' a crimp in their plans, huh? Remember the odds are still two to one in their favour,' muttered Seth.

'Nobody asked you or Wes to join the party, mister,' replied Jeff evenly. 'Just keep outa my way. I owe 'em for Ward....'

'I'm in,' interrupted Wes. 'I reckon they deliberately set me up, so one of 'em must be lookin' fer my scalp anyway. I might just as well meet the *hombre* first as last. We had a saying in the Ninth...'

'Gawd don't let him start on about the war, Jeff,' Seth broke in with a short laugh. 'He'll twist your ear off iffen you give him the chance. Let's just say we're all agreed, it'll save us both a load of earache.'

'One o' these days I'm gonna teach you some respect young fella,' joshed Wes, a wide grin showing off his brilliant white teeth. 'I'm gonna pull down your britches an' paddle your backside like your

mammy should have when you was just a young
shaver.'

'Yeah, you'd better not try it,' laughed Seth as they
turned their mounts along the Chisholm Trail and
lifted them into a lope.

'Reckon to pull off the trail before full dark, find a
place to make camp; my stomach's stuck to my
wishbone,' Jeff said, raising his voice to be heard
above the thrum of hooves.

'Like to try somethin' besides cottontail on a stick,
an' arbuckle instead of water fer a change,' grumbled
Seth. 'An' before you start runnin' off at the mouth,
Wes, don't tell me about what they made you eat
during the goddamned war!'

'Just think of it as a nice juicy steak,' laughed Wes as
Seth groaned in disgust.

In spite of the banter, the men were ever watchful.
They knew that at any moment a roving band of
Indians could come charging out of the surrounding
foothills. So far they had managed to avoid being
spotted. They were all hoping their good fortune
would hold.

Lady Luck was still smiling on them four days later
when they nooned at the Arkansas River close to
where it crossed the Chisholm Trail.

In a few weeks' time the herd would probably
rejoin the trail at this point to continue their journey
towards Abilene, Jeff thought absently.

Although the three men were getting close to the
Kansas border no one was relaxing. It might mean
that they would be out of the Indian Territories but
Kansas was still in a state of turmoil with Indian raids
a regular occurrence.

They were about to mount up when Seth paused
and, shielding his eyes against the glare of the sun,

stared off into the distance. 'Rider comin'. Towin' a pack hoss by the look of it,' he muttered.

Jeff and Wes paused and stared along the banks of the river, waiting expectantly as the rider slowly closed the gap between them.

'Reckon he might be toting some coffee?' asked Seth hopefully.

'What if he is? I don't see him sharing it with us,' replied Wes. 'Anyway, we've kinda gotten used to water now, be a shame to spoil it.'

'It's just a kid,' grunted Jeff. 'D'you reckon it could be young Billy-Joe?'

'Let's go see,' replied Seth, swinging into his saddle.

He was quickly joined by his two companions as they kicked their mounts into a lope.

The diminutive figure ahead drew his mount to a halt, withdrew his rifle from the saddle-boot and pumped the lever as he saw the three men approaching. Then recognition was mutual and he slapped the horse into a run as he gave a joyous whoop of welcome.

'Where the hell did you spring from?' shouted Seth as they dismounted. 'Goddamnit they shouldn't have let a young shaver like you out here on your own, you could have bin scalped or somethin'.'

'That'd be better than what Tyler an' McBride was gonna do to me,' replied Billy-Joe.

'You got any arbuckle in that there pack, fella?' interrupted Wes.

'Yeah, I pilfered some stores before I pulled out. Took the hosses also; weren't no way I was gonna hang around to be shot like Pinter was,' replied Billy-Joe proudly. 'Figgered that if I could find the cattle trail agin I could maybe make it to this here Abilene place I heard 'em talkin' about. I was chased

into the foothills by some Indians at one time.
Figgered I was done for then, but I lost 'em somehow.
Trouble was I discovered that I was lost also. Took
me four days to find the goddamned river. Sure is
good meetin' up with you fellers though.'

'Reckon we should get off the trail,' cautioned Jeff.
'We got water and the kid's got some coffee, so let's
ride back into the hills, light a fire an' talk this thing
out. We don't want a whole slew of Indians breathing
down our necks do we?'

There were quick nods of agreement as they all
mounted and set off at a steady lope towards the
foothills.

Billy-Joe was the centre of attention as the men
drank their coffee and tasted their first slices of
bacon.

'Beats cottontail any time,' murmured Seth, the fat
dribbling down his chin. 'An' that coffee! Why man
that's pure nectar.'

'What's nectar?' asked Billy-Joe.

'Why, arbuckle of course,' grunted Seth, still
chewing vigorously.

'Guess it's about time you told us what's goin' on
back there, Billy,' Jeff interrupted. 'I need to know
what's happening to those cattle.'

'Yeah, I guess so,' replied Billy-Joe importantly.
'Hot damn, but I didn't ever expect to see you *hombres*
again I kin tell you...'

'Just get on with it, son,' interrupted Wes.

'Yeah, well, the trail boss was as mad as hell when
you an' Seth lit out. Was gonna send Virgil Calder
after you. He wanted to go too, you could tell by the
way he kept easin' his gun in an' out of his holster, like
he was gonna shoot the pair of yuh first chance he
got. But then the storm hit, like that last time, only

worse, an' by the time we settled the herd down proper, McBride reckoned it was too late anyway.'

'McBride, huh?' questioned Jeff. 'Not Matt Tyler?'

'Nope, McBride. I figgered it was funny at the time. Anyway, we pressed on to the brandin' grounds, but when we started to get set, Sam Pinter bagan to kick up a fuss. Said as how nobody was gonna steal any cows belonging to the Lazy P while he was around.'

'So what happened?' prodded Jeff.

'OK, I'm gettin' there,' grumbled Billy-Joe. 'Who's tellin' this thing anyway?'

'Just git on with it lad,' grunted Wes.

'Well, like I was about so say. Sam kicked up quite a fuss an' in the end they had Carl an' Bart tie him up. McBride tied him to a hoss an' they rode off together. Some time after sundown McBride came back with the hoss but no Sam. I asked Carl what was goin' on an' he said if I didn't shut my goddamned mouth I'd be takin' a one-way trip myself, an' when I took the saddle offen Pinter's bronc I noticed there was blood on it.'

'So they were gonna start brand blotting huh?' asked Jeff.

'Yeh, I guess so.'

'What brands were they using?'

'Gawd I dunno,' protested Billy. 'I figgered it was time I left so, bein' the cook, I packed me some vittles, borrowed a couple of hosses an' made tracks that very night. Figgered that with two hosses they'd have a hard time catchin' me if they tried it. Guess they thought I didn't stand a chance out here on my own. But my old daddy was a trapper, an' his daddy before him,' he finished proudly.

'Pity you didn't get to know what brands they was gonna use,' muttered Seth.

'Oh yeah? They was talkin' about me like I was already dead an' buried, so I should hang around an' watch?' shouted Billy-Joe. 'Just how big a fool d'you think I am, mister?'

'You did good, Billy,' soothed Jeff. 'Tell me, did you see any other brandin' irons in the cook shack?'

'Nope, only the ones we used at the start of the drive. Your Lazy Bar K, the Lazy P and the Circle C brandin' irons, Tyler's double arrow was with 'em. They was all tied together in a bunch with a wide strip of rawhide. I was all over that cookshack but I didn't see a sign of any others. Beats me how they could change a load of brands like that without any runnin' irons though.'

'Yeah, me also,' replied Jeff thoughtfully. 'But that's what they're gonna do right enough. You heard Sam Pinter say so, huh?'

'Sure as shootin'. He said it clear, an' I seemed the only one besides Pinter to give a damn.'

Jeff carefully smoothed out the sandy soil and flattened it down with his hand. Using a small piece of wood he marked out the brands, one by one.

The Lazy Bar K consisted of a capital K resting on a bar, while the Lazy P was a rather sloppy looking P tilting backwards, with a dragging end where the bottom loop of the P overrides the main bar. The Circle C-connected was made up of a large circle with a small C in its centre, the C connected to the circle by two straight bars running from the top and bottom of the open end of the C.

Finally, the road brand was two arrowheads placed one behind the other, the smaller arrowhead at the back resting within the larger one.

The men studied the brands for a long time, but in the end they all professed themselves baffled. As far as they could see, there was no way these rather difficult brands could be altered.

The thieves dared not put a different brand on the animals; the buyers would never accept the herd because the old brand would show their origin.

The road brand was Tyler's own so it also had to be altered in some way, otherwise everyone would know that the trail boss was directly linked with the theft.

Ranchers would give rustlers very short shrift indeed if they caught them. The nearest tree was often good enough, and if there were no trees handy, a rope around the neck and a fast gallop over rough ground was just as final.

Jeff lay awake a long time thinking about the brand blotting without arriving at a solution.

His turn for watch came around and he didn't need the nudge that Wes gave him. Jeff shook the thoughts away as he melted into the darkness of the night.

It was around three o'clock when he roused Seth who came awake grumbling and grunting. 'Ain't that time already is it?' he queried.

'You know it is,' Jeff muttered. 'On your way, mister.'

Seth shivered in the chill air. 'Why do I always git the coldest bit?'

'It's the safest bit, that's why. Now git!'

Jeff rolled into Seth's warm bedroll and was instantly asleep.

FIFTEEN

The night was waning on a cobalt blue and red skirt when Billy-Joe touched his arm.

Jeff was awake in an instant, aware of the boy's agitation; aware also, of the rich aroma of freshly brewed coffee in the air as he rolled to his feet, gun in hand.

'What is it?' the words were barely above a whisper.

'I can't find Seth,' muttered the boy. 'Figgered to take him a mug of coffee but he ain't nowhere around.' Billy-Joe's voice held a tremble of fear.

Wes came to his feet at the first sound of voices. 'Trouble?'

'Seems like,' muttered Jeff as he drifted, wraith-like out of the camp, only to return a few minutes later. 'Either he's wandered away or we've got trouble. Didn't your daddy ever tell you never to make coffee in the early hours, son? Especially not in Indian country?'

'Allus made it real early with the herd,' protested Billy-Joe.

'Big herd, lots of men is OK lad, never in a small camp. Indians will smell it a mile off. My fault, I should have warned you; figgered you knew.'

The deep cobalt of the morning was turning to scarlet and gold with the sun pushing at the horizon

122

as Jeff, Wes and Billy-Joe quickly cleared the camp-site, saddled the horses and began to lead them slowly through the trees and scrub of the foothills.

Wes was leading and, as he moved around a large boulder he stopped, holding up a cautionary hand before sinking slowly to the ground.

Passing the hackamore to the boy, Jeff moved up beside Wes. They were in the last clump of rocks and from here the ground stretched flat, broken only by the dark brown tracks of the Chisholm Trail.

Wes pointed silently. They didn't need words.

Seth was pegged out, naked as a jaybird, face up to the sun and strapped down with wet rawhide thongs which would shrink and cut in the heat of the sun. Jeff didn't need to look close to know that the eyelids had been cut away. Seth would be a gibbering wreck before evening, dead in two days.

But the Cheyenne wouldn't let it be that easy, they would soak him down with water to keep him alive and prolong the agony, make him scream for death, hoping his friends would attempt a rescue.

Jeff heard a gasp close behind him. Billy-Joe had tethered the horses and had crawled forward to see what the others were looking at. Jeff turned and saw the beginnings of a tear in the boy's eye.

'That's what can happen if you brew coffee in the clear air of the early mornin',' Jeff muttered. 'Go an' fetch me that old Sharps; it's in Seth's saddle-boot. There's a little pouch of cartridges tied to the trigger-guard. Don't lose em, savvy?'

The lad slipped away and returned in moments with the heavy gun. 'We gonna rescue Seth, huh?' he asked hopefully.

'That's what they'd like us to try, son. We'd never make it.'

Jeff flipped open the loading gate, untied the pouch and loaded the gun.

'What yuh gonna do, Jeff? There ain't no Indians to shoot at.' The boy's whisper was pitched high as he tried to brave it out.

'Ain't shootin' at Indians,' grunted Jeff as he slowly lay down on his stomach and sighted the gun.

'Hey you-all can't shoot *Seth*,' wailed the youngster, as he attempted to grab Jeff's shoulder.

A hefty arm wrapped itself around the boy and an equally big hand pressed across his mouth.

'Get it done, Mason,' grunted Wes. 'I got the boy.'

Slate-grey eyes stared dispassionately down the sights. Jeff drew in his breath and held it as he squeezed the trigger. The gun roared. The body gave a convulsive jerk and it was over.

There was a scream of frustrated anger from a dozen throats as the Indians realized they had lost their victim, and a shower of arrows probed the rocks where the tell-tale cloud of smoke hung in the clear morning air.

Billy-Joe was struggling hard and the big man was having his work cut out trying to subdue the youngster with one arm, while keeping his hand over the boy's mouth to stop him yelling his head off.

Jeff stepped in front of the boy, his Colt appearing in his hand as if by magic. Billy-Joe's eyes opened wide as he stared down the barrel of the gun, inches from his forehead.

'Shut it, son, or I'll leave you behind too,' gritted Jeff. 'We'll be lucky to git out of here as it is, an' you ain't helpin'.'

The boy froze.

'You understand, son?' Jeff's voice was uncompromising.

The lad nodded as two big tears rolled down his face.

'Let him go, Wes, reckon he's got enough savvy to keep his goddamned mouth shut now. Cm'on let's get out of here while we've still got a chance.'

Jeff moved swiftly through the foothills, cutting backwards and forwards, over-tracking and wiping out prints. He seemed to be everywhere at once, instantly silencing any comment with a raised hand almost before it was uttered.

Billy-Joe was drooping in the saddle and Wes was not much better as dusk was settling over the land.

They had spent a full day in the saddle by the time Jeff brought them back to the same set of boulders and dismounted.

'What happens now?' grunted Wes.

'We wait until dark. I'll go an' take a good look around to make sure I've lost 'em; keep it quiet Wes, OK?'

Jeff was gone before Wes could reply, An hour later he ghosted around in the deep shadow of the rocks. 'We're in the clear,' he muttered as he came within touching distance of Wes.

'Gawd, I wish you wouldn't keep doin' that!' muttered Wes in a harsh whisper. 'What happens now?'

'Now, we climb aboard an' ride like hell,' Jeff growled. 'With two spare hosses we should be in the clear long before they sort out our tracks an' they won't want to ride at night anyway.'

They hit the saddles on the run, Wes towing one horse and Jeff the other. Being the lightest; Billy-Joe was soon up front. They swept past the darker blob that was Seth Calhoun almost without a glance and turned on to the Chisholm Trail, using it as their guide to Abilene.

With a ten-minute fast run behind them they cut their speed to a lope which gave them time to peer along their back-trail.

'After another hour of steady riding, Wes pulled alongside Jeff.

'That was some right smart tricks you pulled back there.' Wes spat, and wiped the back of his hand across his mouth. 'Done lost me in the first ten minutes. Fooled the war-whoops too by the look of it. Where the hell did you ever learn to out-fox a goddamned Indian?'

'Sioux chief name of Eagle Eye. Was like a second father to me.'

'Figgers,' grunted Wes. 'Takes one to know one I suppose. You reckon we could pull over an' git outside of some grub without causing us any *more* grief? My stomach's beginning to think my throat's bin cut.'

'We'll just keep goin' 'til morning.'

'You ain't *real* man,' replied Wes. 'I could even eat Billy-Joe if there's nothing else on offer.'

'Tomorrow,' replied Jeff succinctly. 'No coffee an' no fire. We should be over the border an' into Kansas by now. Figger to get some real decent grub in the next few days or so.'

'Well glory alleluia to that,' crowed Wes. 'I sure would like to see a good-sized steak, cooked so rare that it's liable to get up an' walk right offen the goddamned plate. Man you-all have got me drooling somethin' awful.'

'What about poor old Seth?' Billy-Joe's doleful voice brought Wes down to earth with a bump.

'Son, I kin understand how you feel, but you gotta realize that everybody don't live to a ripe old age, an' you gotta be real grateful that it ain't you back there starin' at the sky. Seth just wasn't sharp enough to keep ahead of the war-whoops. You just keep your eye on old smarty-pants here; ain't nobody gonna out-fox him I'll wager. But just remember one thing, when a man's dead he's dead, that's a fact an' all the weepin' an' wailin' in the whole world ain't gonna change it.'

'You finished?' grunted Jeff.

'Think so.'

'Thank God. It's no wonder you're always hungry, running off at the mouth like that all the time.'

'Ain't you *the* most grumblin' feller though,' retorted Wes. 'Didn't your daddy ever give you a good talkin'-to?'

'Sure did, he just weren't so long-winded about it. A man could starve to death waitin' for you to get to the point....'

The morning sun was climbing high in the sky and still Jeff had shown no signs of stopping to eat. All three were jogging along dreamily enjoying the warmth after the cold of the night ride.

'Sure am hungry, man,' hinted Wes for the fourth or fifth time.

'How long afore we gits to this Abilene place?' interrupted Billy-Joe.

'About a week or so by my reckoning,' replied Jeff.

'Real settled country hereabouts, huh?'

'That's the way Tyler told it, son.'

'So we shouldn't pay no never mind to that bunch of Indians comin' over the hill behind us, huh?'

On the heels of the question they all heard the unmistakable high-pitched Hi Hi of Indians on the rampage, and after one startled glance over his shoulder, Jeff spurred his mount driving it into a fast gallop with his two companions only a short head behind.

Riding over a high ridge they began to descend into a lush green valley. At the bottom was a small stream and beside it a large, square log cabin with a peaceful-looking curl of smoke drifting from the chimney. A man in dungarees was strolling towards the house carrying an axe in one hand and a rifle in the other.

They raced for the haven at a full gallop. The man stopped and peered in their direction for a second, then headed for the house at a run.

Moments later Jeff and his two companions came to a dust-swirling halt in the yard. The man stuck his head out of the large double doorway, gun in hand.

'Just hold it right there, gents,' he growled. 'I don't take kindly tuh strangers.'

'How d'you feel about Indians?' shouted Wes as the shrill war-cry came again.

'Suppose you'd best come in then,' replied the man grumpily. 'Hosses an all iffen you want to keep 'em.'

The split-log building consisted of one huge room with the back part roped off as a corral, where an ancient horse was contentedly munching some hay. It also contained a couple of goats and stank to high heaven.

Wes loosened one rope and drove the five horses into the makeshift pen before looking around.

The place was built to withstand a siege; there were no windows, only a series of gun slits cut in the logs with a heavy timber flap to cover any that were not in use. The whole of the roof was covered with a thick layer of turf and soil. There were four modern rifles and a shot-gun in a rack by the door with a plentiful supply of ammunition scattered around.

Once the big door was closed and a two-by-four dropped into position the room was in darkness;

apart from the shafts of sunlight cutting through the open gun ports.

'You *hombres* sight-seein' or shootin'?'

'Kin we have a loan of some guns?' asked Wes.

'Take your pick,' replied the nester, around a chaw of tobacco.

'You alone here?' asked Jeff, as he loaded a Spencer carbine.

'D'you see anybody else around?' The man spat at the fire and missed.

'No.'

'Looks like you-all could be right then.' He spat again … and missed. 'Name's Josh. How many Indians?'

'I'm Jeff, this here's Wes an' that's Billy-Joe. Are we in Kansas yet, Josh?'

'Just about, son. How many Indians?'

'Dozen or so. How far to Abilene?'

'About a week's ridin', but it ain't that easy. The Cheyenne bin raidin' all along the border, reckon that'll put a crimp in any plans you might have on reachin' Abilene inside of three weeks. Be sensible to stick around here fer a while. They probably won't even try me fer long; they know I'm a tough nut to crack an' there's easier pickin's out there.' Josh spat for a third time … and missed. 'Never can hit that dad-blasted fire like old Griff could,' he muttered.

'Griff?' asked Jeff. 'Thought you said you was alone?'

'Yeah, am now. The Indians caught Griff, took a fancy to his hair.'

'You got enough grub an' such for us too?' queried Wes hopefully.

'Yup, be kinda glad of the company. Ain't talked so much in a whole goldarned month. Oh, by the way, I also got me a dog, name of Ben. He's out huntin' meat right now, real likeable critter. Just don't stand in his way iffen he's in a hurry, he's like to git uppity.'

He strolled up to one of the gun ports. 'They'm sittin' out there tryin' tuh make up their minds if we-all is worth the bother,' he grunted. 'Let's make up their minds fer 'em.'

The four men opened fire on the waiting Indians. It was enough. They whipped their ponies around and galloped away, one holding a damaged arm.

'Told yuh,' grunted Josh as he slipped the cover over the gun ports one after the other, before opening the doorway.

'Like to bring the hosses out, boys? They kinda mess up the place if they stay in here too long.'

'Air gets kinda heavy, huh?' grinned Billy-Joe as he led them into a small corralled area. 'Won't the Indians steal 'em?'

'Not when Ben gits back they won't. Yonder he comes now, got us some dinner seems like.'

The two men and Billy-Joe watched in amazement as a dog the size of a tiger lumbered into the yard towing a small deer. He placed it on the floor beside his master then turned a jaundiced eye on the strangers, a low growl of warning in the back of his throat.

'You ever put a saddle on him?' asked Wes.

'You like to try?' countered Josh, 'cos I'd sure like to watch.'

He grabbed one of the horns and dragged the deer towards the others. 'Seein' as you're uninvited guests p'raps you'd like to skin 'er out an' cut a few slices fer the pan. Make sure you leave a haunch fer Ben, otherwise he just might get to dislike y-all. Me an' the hound will just take a look around while you git the dinner ready, that sit OK with y-all?'

Without waiting for a reply he snapped his fingers and strolled off with the dog following at his heel.

SIXTEEN

Matt Tyler was worried that Billy-Joe had slipped away but Quincy McBride scoffed at the idea that the boy would ever make it through Indian Territory, much less to Abilene.

'He's long dead by this time,' McBride assured Tyler.

'Like Sam Pinter?' asked the trail boss. 'I tell you, McBride, if I'd known what was involved here I never would have gone along with it in the first place.'

'Just think of how much money you're gonna make once we git to Abilene,' replied Quincy. 'That'll kill your doubts.'

'What about Virgil Calder? Or is he your boss?'

'He's going along with it. Thinks he's gonna git a share … some hopes eh?' McBride gave a snigger. 'His share will come outa the barrel of a forty-five. An' like I told you; don't git curious, savvy? Now that all the brand blotting's finished we kin start back along the river, huh? I gotta say, Tyler, you sure are a dab hand with a runnin' iron an' a wet blanket. Real slick work, nobody'll be able to tell those dogies have been blotted the way you did it.'

'Yeah, well I've had some practice,' grunted Tyler, slightly mollified by the praise. 'I've also done some scouting around here. 'Pears that we could cut across country at an angle an' head direct into Abilene instead of following the river back to the Chisholm Trail. Save us about a week in trailing time. We'll miss the main trail an' come in from the east, save around a hundred and fifty miles or so.'

'Wa-al now that's a great idea,' applauded McBride. 'Quicker we kin sell the herd an' git our hands on all that *dinero* the better. So we'll be gettin' under way tomorrow, right?'

Tyler nodded and McBride walked away, his harsh barking laugh showing his good humour at the news.

The trail boss stared at McBride's back, his mind turning over the possibilities. With Sam Pinter dead and McBride talking about killing Calder, the only people remaining were himself, McBride and the Simes brothers. So maybe there *was* an extra player in the game that he knew nothing about. One of the ranchers perhaps? Or was McBride playing it really cagey?

Tyler shrugged. He would soon know. Matt stared with quiet pride at the new brands; he'd never seen better. Already the scars were healing and in a few days no one would be able to tell that the brands had been altered....

At first light the herd was on the move, fording the Arkansas River and heading across country into Kansas.

With only five drovers the going was hard and the men were riding backwards and forwards continuously, making sure there were no stragglers and keeping the animals lined out at easy walking pace.

Fortunately, over the weeks the beasts had become used to the trail and were now content to plod gently along.

The weather was kind and, for a change, the skyline was free of Indians. It was hell on the horses but there was a large remuda, each man having had originally at least six remounts. The loss of five of the original riders had increased the spare riding stock, so as fast as one horse became exhausted another was saddled and set to work.

By the end of each day, however, the men were hardly able to stand up. On night guard the men slept in their saddles leaving their mounts to continue the endless circling of the herd from instinct alone.

There was no shortage of meat or water, but bacon, coffee and other staple foods were just about finished. It had been short rations ever since the first stampede had smashed the chuck wagon, and the supply had been cut even more when young Billy-Joe sloped off with a substantial portion of what was left.

Conversation was cut to a minimum. A curt 'Yeah' or 'No' was about as much as Tyler could expect in answer to a question. The men would have been at each other's throats at the slightest provocation, but they were too bone weary to bother.

They started to perk up however when they saw the first signs of civilization three weeks after leaving the Arkansas, a cluster of farm buildings in the distance.

Matt Tyler rode ahead promising to try to obtain some coffee and bacon from the farm, but as the men came closer they could see that the buildings had been raided by Indians. Bodies still lay rotting in the yard where they had fallen. Stale smoke was spooking the steers so the men pushed them along as quickly as they could.

Tyler rode up beside McBride. 'That's why we haven't had an Indian problem,' he grunted. 'Must have bin a big raidin' party.'

'How far to Abilene now d'you reckon?' asked McBride.

'I hope to be ridin' into town late tomorrow to get the pens ready,' answered Tyler. 'We'll find some good ground ahead an' bed the herd down 'til I know there's room. I'll send some decent chowder out to you as soon as I get in, OK?'

McBride nodded. 'I'll let the men know. Don't be too long with that grub, huh? An' you'd best send out a few extra drovers, with guns, in case the war-whoops come back. Besides, if things work out the way it was planned we'll be ridin' in with a complete new crew … if you get my meanin',' he added with a sly wink.

Tyler was still trying to come to terms with what was going to happen to the Simes brothers, and maybe Calder too. He just grunted an uneasy acknowledgement.

'Don't forget, Tyler, if a buyer's interested make sure the herd is credited to Major Alan Smithe. With an E. Savvy?'

'I know,' replied Matt wearily. 'We've gone over this a dozen times already.'

'Yeah, just don't forget it,' grumbled McBride. 'You get goin', I'll take care of things here.'

'An' I know how,' sneered Tyler. 'So long, McBride.'

SEVENTEEN

Jeff Mason, Wesley Calvin and Billy-Joe made three attempts to leave the nester's home and head for Abilene, but each time, they were driven back by the Cheyenne, who seemed determined not to let anyone escape from the log fortress.

'They kin pen me in here for as long as they like just so's the grub's good,' remarked Wes, with a big grin after the third abortive attempt. 'Trouble is, McBride an' Tyler must be close to Abilene by this time; unless they've lost their hair. Those Indians are really on the prod, huh, Jeff?'

Mason nodded as he stared grimly out of a gunport. 'Come hell or high water I'm going at full dark tonight.' His voice brooked no argument. 'You two can please yourselves whether you come along. I'm going.'

'How about Josh?' Wes glanced at the elderly man who waved a deprecating hand.

'Don't fret yourself about me, boys, I was here before you came.' He spat at the fire ... and missed. 'Be here if you happen to drop by in a year or so I reckon. Me an' Ben ain't goin' no place.'

'I'm going tonight, any takers?' Jeff looked at Wes who nodded. 'Gettin' to smell kinda high in here, figger we'd best be movin'.' Jeff turned to Billy-Joe.

'Maybe you should hang on here with Josh, son.'

'Hell, no, I'm a' comin' too, Jeff,' replied the boy stoutly. 'I'm wantin' to see this here Abilene place, so count me in.'

Jeff shrugged. 'Your choice fella.' And to Josh, 'You reckon you'll make out OK?'

'Like I said, son, don't worry about me. Just you pull out when you're ready, Ben an' me kin take care of a few Indians, huh, Ben?'

The dog growled reassuringly.

Later that night, before the moon rose, they opened the big double doors and slipped away, walking their horses for the first mile or so before easing into the saddle and riding at a steady lope.

They managed to keep out of sight of the marauding bands of Indians and, as they drew nearer the town, so the dangers decreased.

Trail-weary, dirty and unkempt, especially Jeff, with his knife-torn shirt, a grimy pair of moccasins, no hat and a dirty-looking red bandanna tied around his throat.

The place was not much more than a village doing its best to look like a town. This was the first year that trail herds had been coming to Abilene. The huge new split-rail stock pens were twice the size of the town itself, and every pen was full of bawling bellowing cattle.

People were almost crawling over each other in their haste to get somewhere else. Abilene seemed ready to burst at the seams.

Billy-Joe stared in open-mouthed amazement, 'Je-willickers,' he muttered. 'I ain't never seen so many people in my life, not all in one place anyway,' he amended.

There was a sudden disturbance along the street;

some shouting, followed by a flurry of gunshots. By the time the three rode by it was over and two dead men lay in the street. People hurrying by did not even glance at the bodies.

'Nice place,' muttered Jeff.

'This is nothin',' replied Wes airily. 'Why I remember once, during the war that is...'

'You sure can flap that lip of yours,' interrupted Jeff with a grin.

The grin was suddenly wiped from his face. 'Looky yonder, Wes, you ever see those two rannies before?'

'Well now, what d'you know,' muttered Wes. 'The Simes brothers as I live an' breathe.'

Wes made to turn his mount towards them but Jeff stopped him with a hand on his arm.

He looked questioningly at his companion.

'They can probably lead us to McBride an' the others, Wes, so let's not be in too much of a hurry, *amigo*.'

The three pulled up at a hitching rail and tied their mounts. Then, crossing the street, they eased along through the crowd keeping the brothers in sight, both men instinctively easing their guns in their holsters.

Suddenly a pair of batwing doors flew open and two brawling men fell into the crowd, kicking and cursing. By the time Jeff and Wes had managed to push through the milling throng the Simes brothers had vanished.

'Looks like we've lost 'em,' muttered Wes in frustration.

'They'll be around,' replied Jeff. 'It's a small town. Maybe we should ride out to the stock pens an' take a look around. Our herd must be penned up some-where close.'

'Yeah. Gosh almighty. Them pens sure seem to go

on forever.' Billy-Joe was bubbling in his excitement.

'Gonna take some time to look that lot over,' agreed
Jeff. 'An' God knows how many is still grazing out
there waiting for room in the pens. Still, it might be
an idea to try to find who's in charge; they should be
able to point us towards our herd.'

Wes jingled some coins in his pocket. 'Let's eat
first,' he pleaded. 'Goddamn but I'd sure like to
hog-tie a nice juicy steak with all the trimmin's.' He
sniffed appreciatively. 'Man oh man, just breathe
deep on that wonderful smell.'

'OK, OK,' Jeff chuckled. 'You lead, we'll follow.'

It was over an hour later when they headed back to
their horses, climbed aboard and jogged out of the
small township towards the pens.

A train was being loaded so they rode over to check
on the brands. One man seemed to be in charge so
Jeff dismounted and approached him.

Before he could speak the man snapped a look at
him. 'You want somethin', mister?' he growled.

'Yeah,' replied Jeff. 'Who's the boss around here?'

'You're lookin' at him. So?'

'Lookin' for a trail herd. Arrived real recent.
Double arrow road brand. Herd made up from three
different owners. Seen it?'

'Who's askin?' The man was surly at the
interruption.

'I am, somethin' bother you about that?'

The man turned, his hand dropping instinctively to
his holstered pistol. 'Maybe, maybe not; you an owner
or just shootin' the breeze?' Jeff's level stare seemed
to unsettle him. He slowly moved his hand away from
his holster. 'No offence, mister. I'm kinda busy just
now.'

'Answer the question an' I'm on my way,' replied

Jeff affably. 'You want to argue the point, we'll do it that way.'

'Herd came in two days ago, from the east.'

'Not the Chisholm Trail?' Jeff sounded surprised.

'I *said* east, mister. You deaf or somethin'?' The man was becoming more truculent by the minute but Jeff chose to ignore it.

'How many brands?'

'Three.'

'How many head?'

'What the hell is this? You the law or somethin'?'

'Or somethin',' replied Jeff. 'So tell me, how many head, an' make it fast.'

'Nigh on three thousand. Three brands, Boxed Diamond. Double loop an' Double Circle-Cross, with Two Diamonds as a road brand, one inside the other. That satisfy you?'

'Owner?' Jeff's voice was implacable.

'A Major Alan Smithe.'

Jeff's shoulders sagged.

'Not what you wanted to hear huh?' the man fleered, gaining some small satisfaction from Jeff's manner. He began to fidget again when the young man in front of him slowly raised his head. Those slatey blue-grey eyes seemed to pin him like a fly to a fence.

'Trail boss?'

'Name of Walker. We ain't had any other herds in recent, not around that size anyway.'

'Paid by bank draft?'

'Mind your own damned business,' snarled the man.

'Healthier to tell him,' murmured Wes, who had strolled over to see what was happening.

The straw boss whirled to face the voice, his hand dropping to his pistol.

'Why damn you, you're just a N....'

'Don't say it. Don't even think it,' purred Wes. 'Lessen you're ready to die for one leetle word ... white boy.' His voice dripped pure venom.

'Take it easy, Wes, I bin pushing him kinda hard,' soothed Jeff. His voice hardened. 'Bank draft?'

'Yeah, now get out an' leave me be, I got work tuh do.' The sweat pouring down his face was not only from the heat of the day as he slouched away.

'Looks like the herd ain't in yet,' piped Billy-Joe.

'It's in,' grunted Wes. 'Tyler wouldn't let the Simes brothers leave the cattle. They were already short-handed. Let's take a look at this herd the straw boss was talkin' about....'

Dusk was settling in by the time they had located the herd but even in the poor light they could see the Boxed Diamond brand, the Double Loop and Double Circle-Cross.

They edged in for a closer look but they had not been riding around the cattle for many minutes before two cowboys rode slowly towards them.

'Howdy fellers,' greeted one cautiously. 'Somethin' we kin do for you?'

'Looking is all,' replied Jeff. 'You ride for the owners?'

'Naw, trail boss, name of Walker.'

'You bring 'em all the way from Texas?'

'Not this herd. Brought one in a few weeks ago. Me an' Jess here went broke in a card game so we hired on with Walker as cow nurses till they git 'em into the pens.'

'Mind if I take a look at 'em?' asked Jeff.

'Just so long as you don't try tuh hide one under your vest when you leave, we don't give a damn, do we Ted?' laughed Jess.

'Anybody still here from the old crew? My twin brother was supposed to be comin' up from Texas with a herd; like to find him if I can.' Billy-Joe's eyes were wide and innocent.

'Last one left this mornin'. Name of Calder. Too old to be your brother though, young-un,' laughed Ted as the two turned their ponies away to continue circling the herd. 'Mr Walker is due back just after sundown. Don't let him catch y-all hangin' around, could lose us our jobs, OK?'

'A few minutes is all we need; thanks, friend,' replied Jeff as the two rode slowly away into the dusk.

'We ain't got much time,' grunted Wes as they eased their way into the herd. 'Let's take a close look at those brands, an' get out quick.'

They looked at each of the three brands in turn. Billy-Joe seemed more interested than the other two as he ran his small hand over one brand after the other before eventually they rode off in the darkening night.

'Damned if I kin figger it,' grunted Wes. 'All branded up right an' proper. If that cow waddy hadn't mentioned Virgil Calder I'd swear we were lookin' at the wrong herd.'

'Me too,' muttered Jeff.

'Not me,' piped up Billy-Joe. 'I figger I know how it was done. My daddy done told me about all sorts of things. Like how they used to use a runnin' iron on wet-backs out of Mexico. Usin' a hot iron an' a wet blanket he could make a brand look like somethin' altogether different.'

'This ain't one of your windies is it, young feller?' asked Wes severely. 'Time fer pulling tricks is past.'

'It's a neat trick OK,' assured Billy-Joe, loftily. 'But it's as true as kin be. All you have to do is to figger out a mark that the one on the cow kin be changed to, then you use a hot iron an' a wet blanket to change it. Simple!'

'A man could get hanged fer doin' that,' muttered Wes.

'Most of 'em was. My pa was smarter. Gave it up before he got caught, showed me how it went though. Give you some lessons if you like.'

'Don't you get to be no smarty-pants on me, young-un,' replied Wes in false anger. 'Reckon we've got a full-blown criminal here, Jeff.'

'Yeah. What with a Wanted flier out on you, an' now a midget rustler, I'm sure keepin' bad company right enough. My daddy warned me about people like you.'

'Wonder who this Major Smithe is?' asked Wes. 'He's up to his neck in this business, claiming the herd belongs to him. It sure is a puzzle an' no mistake.'

'A good meal an' a night's sleep is what we need,' replied Jeff. 'We'll start to sort this out at first light tomorrow.'

'A good meal? I'm with you all the way, man,' laughed Wes, as he spurred away.

'Thought you would be,' replied Jeff as he rode to catch up. 'Come on, son. Rattle that old bag of bones or you'll miss seein' the wild animal bein' fed....'

EIGHTEEN

Jeff awakened to the smell of freshly brewed coffee mixed with the smell of hay and horses. He rolled over and stared at Billy-Joe who seemed engrossed in something he was scratching in the loose sand on the stable floor.

Jeff climbed to his feet, stretched to remove the kinks and strolled over to the lad.

'Mornin',' he mumbled. 'Where's Wes?'

'Didn't come back last night, remember? He said he was gonna see the sights.'

Jeff poured a mug of arbuckle, scalding hot and thick enough to float a horseshoe. 'You make good coffee, Billy-Joe,' he murmured, as he sipped appreciatively. 'Did the hostler know you made it?'

'He weren't around at the time,' replied the lad with a sly grin. 'But he was happy enough to drink some when I offered it.'

'You're a born outlaw,' chuckled Jeff. 'Wonder what Wes found so interestin'. Place don't seem big enough to use all night for a look-see.'

He glanced down at the drawings in the sand. 'You still figgerin' about the brand business?'

'Don't have to any more. I already got it figgered.'

Jeff crouched beside the lad. 'So, show me how it goes,' he grunted.

'Well I figger it goes like this.' Billy-Joe quickly drew the three brands in the dusty sand.

'See, if you use the same irons, I figger you kin change all the brands. Take the Lazy Bar K. If you turn the iron upside down and reburn it a second time, you make a Boxed Diamond. Then the Circle C-connected. Cut off the circle an' it leaves a C with the two bars stickin' out. Turn it around and add two small lines an' you git the Double Circle-Cross. Then take the Lazy P iron an' brand on a second P, one above t'other, an' you git a Double Loop brand.'

'Well I'll be damned,' muttered Jeff. 'That's real clever thinkin', son. Can you read or write?'

'No sir, but I know brands an I kin mostly read 'em too, but I can't string words together on paper nor read em neither.'

'You're either gonna grow up to be one very smart *hombre* or a goddamned rustler, feller.'

'Yeah, well, I guess you already seen that if you turn the double arrow road brand t'other way it makes the Two Diamonds, an' my daddy told me that if you use a hot iron an' a wet blanket, in a few days you can't even see the joins lessen you skin the animal and look at the hide on the inside. Good huh?'

'Good ... if you're a thief,' muttered Jeff. 'Let's go find Wes. We'll spend the last of our *dinero* on some breakfast before we go an' sort out these damned rustlers.'

'Where are we gonna look for Wes?'

'At this time of day?' scoffed Jeff. 'A hash house, where else?'

'Yeah I should have guessed,' grinned Billy-Joe, as they made for the stable door. 'I done good with the brands though, huh?'

'You sure did, son. Never would have figgered it

out myself.' He dropped a fatherly hand on the boy's shoulder. 'Just make sure you don't let it drag you to the wrong side of the tracks. All that know-how could be a big temptation but it could leave you on the wrong end of a rope.'

'Yeah, it sure could. Ain't likely though, I wanna be a cowboy not a rustler. Let's eat, huh?'

There seemed to be even more people crowding the street this morning, cowboys jostling with frock-coated businessmen, and bonneted women with their shopping baskets on their arms, mingled with strong-smelling buffalo hunters and trappers. It was as if someone had kicked an anthill.

They were attempting to ease their way past a small group of gossiping women when Jeff happened to glance across the crowded roadway.

He caught a brief glimpse of Wesley Calvin, strolling along beside Virgil Calder. But before he could shout or cross the road, two large wagons laden with huge logs, each towed by four horses cut across his vision and by the time they had passed, the two men had gone.

'Did you see that, Billy?'

'Can't see nothin',' grunted the boy. 'I'm too small, what was it, Jeff?'

'Could have sworn I saw Wes talking to Calder.' He shook his head.

'Ain't likely is it, Jeff?'

'No, I must have bin mistaken. C'mon son let's find a hash house....'

After they had finished their breakfast, Jeff and Billy-Joe wandered through the throng for over two hours without meeting up with Wes.

'Beats me where he could be,' grunted Jeff.

They were standing on a raised walkway leaning

against the wall of a dry-goods store. From here they could see over the heads of the crowds in the roadway to scan the boardwalk, opposite.

Billy-Joe saw Jeff stiffen and ease himself off the wall.

'Trouble?' he asked.

'Maybe time to get some answers,' replied Jeff as he allowed his hands to caress the butts of his Colts. 'I kin see Matt Tyler an' one of the Simes brothers across the way. I'm gonna have me a talk with those *hombres*, you keep looking for Wes.'

Without waiting for a reply, Jeff stepped off the boardwalk and drifted into the crowded roadway making his way at an angle to intercept the two men.

They were still some distance ahead when Jeff saw them turn into a side alley.

Slipping and dodging through the crowd Jeff made good time to the corner. Easing cautiously around it he saw the two men about halfway down the alley. Unlike the street the alley was empty except for the two men, who were strolling along side by side, deep in conversation.

Jeff rapidly but silently closed the gap. But the men seemed to be aware of his presence, because they both turned together, hands poised above flared six-guns.

'Well, howdy, Mason,' grunted Carl Simes, showing no surprise. 'Thought you was dead.'

'Then you made a bad mistake, mister,' gritted Jeff. 'You can try when you're ready.'

'You think you kin take all four of us?' asked Tyler with a sneering grin.

'Yeah, that's right, four of us,' sniggered McBride from behind. 'Ain't that so, Bart?'

'Sure is. We spotted you on the walk back there, Mason. I don't know how the hell you made it out there in Indian country, but right now you ain't got a snowball's chance in hell.'

Whipsawed! Jeff's mind screamed. They'd baited a trap and he had fallen for it like a yearling in his eagerness.

His mind honed in on the two in front of him. 'They might get me but you kin be damned sure you two won't be around to crow about it,' Jeff hissed. 'I'm ready when you are.'

His mind was tuned to every sound behind him, waiting for the tell-tale sound of metal against leather.

Faintly he heard the musical tune of jinglebobs. He was hearing things. He had to be!

Then he heard the slap and clack of a bullet being jerked into a rifle.

'These two will be easy, son. Leave you with the two in front ... if they still want to die. I'm Captain Luke Malloy, an officer of the law, fellers, if y-all wanna drop the gun belts an' talk this thing through, OK. If not ... make your play.'

The four men had recovered from the shock of having the play turned against them and they wanted no truck with the law. The two men in front of Jeff crouched and drew.

Mason had already assessed that the trail boss would be the slower of the two as his hands blurred into a movement too fast for the eye to follow.

Carl was fast, but his guns were hardly out of their holsters before his mouth shaped into a small round ooh of pain as a .45 slug tore into his gut. The second ball tore off the top of his head as he fell into it.

Behind him Jeff heard the double-spaced bark of Malloy's Winchester .66 'Yellow Boy' as his own Colt centred on Tyler's chest.

Matt Tyler's gun was up and pointing.

The hammer lifted and fell twice under the pressure of Jeff's thumb and Tyler's vest puffed dust as the two leaden slugs knocked him off his feet, leaving him sprawled in the alleyway.

Jeff crouched and turned in one fluid motion, but there was nothing to do: Quincy McBride and Bart Simes were as dead as they'd ever be, and Luke was standing over them, as smart as ever in his immaculate pearl-grey vest, with creased pants tucked into the tops of polished riding boots, his matching stetson set at just the right tilt. The 'Yellow Boy' looked tiny in his big capable hands.

At the far end of the alley Jeff noticed the diminutive figure of Billy-Joe, coming as fast as his legs could carry him.

'Jumpin' Jiminy,' the boy yelled, his voice pitched high with adolescent excitement. 'I ain't seen nothin' to match that in all my born days.'

He skidded to a halt beside the tall stranger and looked him up and down.

'Hell, ain't he dressed to kill though, Jeff. You goin' a'partyin' mister?' His voice was still screechingly high.

''Pears as how you ain't bin taught any manners, sonny,' growled Luke, as he grabbed a prominent ear and drew the boy close. 'Take a long look, son, this is how a man *should* keep himself.'

He released the ear and his nose twitched.

'How come I always find you lookin' like a goddamned scarecrow an' stinking to high heaven, Mason?' he asked.

'How the hell did you manage to find me anyway, Luke?'

'Sheer luck. I was standin' in my room at The

Drovers opposite, watchin' the crowds, when I saw this scruffy feller, lookin' like a left-over from a mountain lion's dinner step into the road. Had a dirty red bandanna tied around his neck so I knew it had to be you. Then I saw you were following two fellers who turned into this here alley. Right behind you two more *hombres* turned in; figgered it had to mean trouble an' hot-footed over.'

He turned to Billy-Joe. 'You know, sonny, last time I met him he looked just like he does now, and stink! You'd never believe it. I kitted him out an' paid fer two baths. He looked a picture, but look at him now. As bad as when he started, an' all he had to do was to bring a few measly cows to Abilene.'

He slipped his hand into a well-tailored trouser pocket. 'No money I'll bet!'

Jeff grinned. 'Nope.'

Malloy produced a handful of dollars and passed them to his friend. 'Get cleaned up, and the urchin too. Get some new gear, an' Jeff...'

'I know,' grinned Jeff. 'No scent in the bath water, right?'

'Right!' laughed Luke. 'Look me up at The Drovers hotel when you're clean an' tidy. You can give me the low-down on these *hombres* then. OK?'

Luke touched the brim of his hat lightly with the barrel of the Winchester. 'See you-all later,' he said, as he strolled away with the rifle resting on his shoulder, the faint tinkle of the jinglebobs fading as he left the alley.

'Who the hell was *that*?' asked Billy-Joe wonderingly, as he stared after the departing figure.

'A very good friend, Billy, just hope that one day you have friends like him.'

'Goddamn I sure hope so,' muttered the lad. 'He

just up an' gave you more dollars than I ever seen in my whole life, an' for nothin' too.'

Jeff grinned. 'It's more than that, son,' he murmured, as they walked towards the road. 'He's the kind of friend that's always there when the chips are down, and that's mighty important. Now, let's go an' do like the man said, then we'll take another look for Wes. Sure can't figger out where he's got to.'

'Yeah. Say Jeff, what the hell's a urchin?'

'A dirty scruffy kid whose clothes is more holey than righteous, an' stinks to boot.'

'Like you?'

'Yeah, but I ain't no kid.'

'Three out of four ain't bad an' I'll get to be older,' grinned Billy-Joe proudly. 'Man, but you sure can flick a mean gun, Jeff. Like you to teach me sometime. OK?'

Jeff grinned, 'One day maybe. We'll see,' he promised.

It was several hours later and Jeff and Billy-Joe were sitting in the lobby of The Drovers. They had told Luke about the rustling attempt over a glass or two of root beer.

'So what's happened to this Calvin feller an' Calder?' asked Luke.

'Hard to figger,' replied Jeff. 'Sure ain't nowhere in this burg. We've hunted everywhere at least twice.'

'An' you don't know this Major Alan Smithe neither?'

'Never heard of him. All I know is the bank draft was made out to him, an' although the steers have different brands right now, they're the same ones we choused up from Texas. Billy-Joe showed you how the brands were altered.'

'Yeah, smart young fella ain't he?' Luke waved an

admonitory finger at the grinning lad. 'Don't you go leadin' my friend into bad ways, sonny, or I'll tan your hide good. You hear me?'

Billy-Joe nodded still grinning. 'No sir,' he replied. 'I surely won't.'

'Let's mosey down to the bank an' see if this Major Smithe has cashed the banker's draft yet. Even if he has, we might get a description from the teller,' grunted Luke as they finished their drinks and strolled into the street.

The Cattleman's Bank was not large but it was very busy. Everything spoke of the sudden upturn in business since the trail herds had started coming to Abilene.

They waited patiently at the counter until their turn came around, then Luke flashed his ranger badge at the teller.

'Captain Malloy,' he said loudly. 'Like to see the manager if you please.'

They were quickly directed to a small office with the name R.S. Slade on the door.

A large florid individual glared at the three from behind an overly large desk.

'Understand a banker's draft made out to a Major Alan Smithe was deposited here, I want to know if it's been cashed, Mr Slade,' Luke asked politely.

'Mind your own damned business,' snapped the manager. 'Let me see this badge you waved at my teller.'

Luke pulled the badge from his pocket. 'I'm Captain Malloy. Texas Rangers.'

Slade leaned back in his padded chair and steepled his fingers, a supercilious smile pasted on his face. 'A Johnny Reb huh?' He made it sound like a swear word. 'As you are no doubt aware, *Mister* Malloy,' – he made that sound like a swear word too – 'you have no jurisdiction outside of Texas. You will also know that the Texas Rangers have been disbanded in favour of a new policing method. What have you to say about that?'

'I just want to know if the banker's draft has been cashed.'

'Well I am not going to tell you....'

The smile froze as Jeff cocked his sixgun. 'Then tell *me*, mister, I ain't got time to mess around an' you ain't got much time either.'

The manager suddenly started to perspire. His hand dropped to his trouser pocket for his handkerchief.

'Don't!' growled Jeff, putting a false harshness into his voice.

The man fluttered his hand. 'Just reaching for my handkerchief is all,' he croaked.

'Answer the question or you won't need it,' Jeff's tone was uncompromising.

Slade fidgeted with some papers on the desk. He made two attempts to speak before he managed it. 'You give me a reason why I should, apart from that pistol, and I'll try to help,' he mumbled, swallowing painfully.

'Could help to stop a rustler gettin' away with the proceeds of three thousand head of cattle,' broke in Malloy persuasively.

The manager cleared his throat with considerable effort. 'We-el, in that case, I can tell you that it was *not* cashed. The money has been transferred by letter of credit to another bank.'

'Which one?' asked Luke.

'I'm not sure if I should tell you that,' murmured Slade, 'but I will,' he added hurriedly as Jeff reached for his pistol a second time. 'It's a bank in a small settlement named Dodge. Close to the Indian Territory.'

'And you have no idea what this Major Smithe looks like?'

'No, I'm sorry.' The banker seemed to relent on his earlier abruptness. 'I hope you manage to put matters to rights,' he mumbled as the men headed for the door.

Once outside they hurried to the stables and collected their horses. Jeff left Luke and Billy-Joe to buy the supplies while he rode around the township taking a last look for Wesley Calvin and Virgil Calder.

By the time Jeff returned to the stables, Luke had used one of the spare mounts as a pack horse; it was loaded and they were ready to ride. Calvin's horse had been saddled in case he had returned.

'No luck then?' asked Luke.

'Nope,' replied Jeff, as he drew to a halt. 'Beats me where he could have gone. Didn't have any money to speak of. No horse either. I've even bin out to the loading pens. He just ain't in Abilene, an' we can't wait around; I wanna be there when this Smithe *hombre* tries to cash his note.'

They pulled away in a swirl of dust, heading back towards the Indian Territory. Jeff was glad to leave the noise and bustle of Abilene behind him but he was still puzzled about Calvin's disappearance.

NINETEEN

Wesley Calvin rode slumped in the saddle. He was unarmed, with his manacled hands bound to the saddle-horn and his feet strapped together with a rope tied under the horse's belly.

Virgil Calder rode a few paces ahead. The reins of Calvin's mount tied to his saddle to prevent any attempt at escape.

A loaded pack horse was tied to the rear of Calvin's saddle.

Wes stared glumly at Calder's back. He'd fallen for the bounty-hunter's spiel when he had accidentally met the man on the street in Abilene.

It was great to meet up with him again, Calder told him with seeming sincerity and they spent the rest of the night on the town at Calder's expense. Somewhere along the line he had passed out.

Next morning Wes had awakened with the grandaddy of all hangovers and as Calder seemed to be in the same state they decided on a drop of the hard stuff to wash away the cobwebs before they breakfasted together.

With a good meal inside him, Wes was feeling in an expansive mood. He told Calder about Jeff and Billy-Joe. Even offered to take him along to meet them.

Calder had seemed surprised and shocked to know they were still around. It should have warned him, Wes thought sourly.

They had turned into an alley to take a short cut to the stables and that's when the lights went out.

When he came out of it he was manacled, strapped to a strange bronc and on his way out of town, heading for a place called Dodge because the bounty hunter had some business to take care of there.

Wes had a raging thirst, the legacy of a night of drinking, a head that felt as if a herd of cows had run over it and a deep burning sensation in his gut.

'Any chance of a drink?' he called hoarsely.

Calder stopped and drew Calvin's horse up beside him. He cast a critical eye over his prisoner. 'You look like shit,' he said unfeelingly as he uncorked his canteen and held it to Calvin's lips. 'Don't want you dying on me yet, fella. It's a long way to Arkansas. You'd be so rotten time I got you there they'd never pay the bounty.'

He took a short swig from the canteen and spat it out before taking a longer drink. 'Don't get any ideas though.' Calder grinned as he replaced the stopper and wiped an arm across his mouth. 'I bin a bounty hunter fer a long time; nobody ever got away once I had 'em. You try an' I'll kill you without thinkin' twice about it. Take your scalp back an' try to get the money thataway if I have to. I don't give up on ten thousand dollars that easily.'

'So why bother to go to Dodge? Seems to me you're takin' a hell of a long way round.'

Calder winked. 'That's my business. Lot of money to be made in Dodge ... if you know where to look. C'mon, let's move it, we ain't got forever.'

'Yeah?' snapped Calvin defiantly. 'You got less time

than you know. Mason don't give up on his friends. He'll be along any time now.'

The moment the words were out of his mouth Wes regretted it.

A thoughtful frown pasted itself on the bounty hunter's face. 'Yeah, you're right,' he muttered. 'Best take care of that little problem.'

He pulled the horses off the trail and headed for a stand of trees and boulders. Within moments he had tied his prisoner to a tree and herded the horses out of sight. Then taking his rifle he settled down at a point where the rocks drifted down to the marked trail and waited....

It took three hours, waiting with the patience of an Indian before Calder saw the dust of three riders moving rapidly towards him.

He hadn't expected three but, what the hell, he thought, as he sighted on the one nearest to him.

The Henry rifle spat once and the man left the saddle as if he'd run into a wall. Before he could even draw a second bead, the other man was leaning over his mount like an Indian, making a weaving run directly towards his hiding-place.

Disconcerted by the fast reaction he fired two quick shots which missed. The man was closing fast. Calder could see the cocked six-gun in his fist. In thoughtless panic he came up to a crouch to get a better shot.

The six-gun beat a three-shot tattoo. The first clipped his shoulder jerking Calder to his feet, the second buried itself into his stomach. He didn't feel the third, his throat was just not up to that kind of punishment.

Wes heard the shooting and started yelling his head off. It was Billy-Joe who found him, cut him free and found the key to the manacles in Calder's vest pocket.

Jeff was kneeling beside Luke. All other considera-
tions were washed out of his mind. His friend had
taken a bullet in the chest but he was not unconscious.

'Why is it that every time I git tangled up with you I
git hurt somehow?' Luke groaned, as Jeff, helped by
Wes, made him as comfortable as possible in the
shade of the trees.

Jeff crouched beside his friend and checked on the
heavy flesh wound. 'You won't be riding for a few
days,' he murmured. 'I don't like doin' it, pardner,
but I'm gonna have to leave you with Wes. I've got to
git to Dodge real fast. You understand that don't
you?'

'Sure,' murmured Luke, 'from what Wes has told
us, somebody is gonna collect a wad of *dinero* in
Dodge an' that bounty hunter was about to collect his
share. You ride feller, take the boy with you, an' send
him back with a buckboard real soon, huh?'

Jeff patted his shoulder. 'Leave it with you, Wes;
we'll get back as soon as maybe, OK? So long.'

Jeff and Billy-Joe swung into their saddles and
rode off at a gallop.

They rode fast, all day and far into the night before
taking a brief rest to allow the horses to eat and drink
at a small stream. By sundown they were approaching
Dodge.

Men and horses were practically dead on their feet
as, almost falling off their mounts, they crawled into
the livery. The stable-man could see their plight and
allowed them to doss down in his cubby-hole. He even
gave them coffee and a chunk of soda bread apiece in
exchange for a half-dollar.

Billy-Joe was awake early the next morning, his
youthful body quickly adjusting to the rigours of the
last two days.

Eager to see the sights, he slipped out of the stables and made a tour of the small township. The local eatery was already open and the smell of fresh-brewed coffee and the tantalizing smell of bacon coaxed him in. He had two dollars in his pocket that Jeff had given him so he sauntered up to the counter and bought himself a breakfast.

Having completed his meal, he was wiping his mouth on his bandanna as he got up to leave. A man pushed open the door and strolled up the counter.

Billy-Joe stopped dead in his tracks, his eyes bugged out in shock. This man was dead!

Billy backed out of the doorway keeping the bandanna to his face. Then he turned and ran.

Being a boy he could not help shouting for Jeff at the top of his voice as he ran.

The man at the counter turned and recognized Billy-Joe running hell for leather towards the end of town. He spun on his heels and left the hash house. Outside, he swung into his saddle and set the horse at a lope, quickly overhauling the boy.

Turning the horse side on to the boy his hand dipped to his right-hand sixgun.

The bullet tore into Billy's back, punching him to the ground.

The man touched spurs to his mount and galloped down an alley between two stores.

Billy-Joe lay where he had fallen. No one ventured out to see what the shooting was about. No one cared.

Slowly, painfully, the boy dragged himself to his feet, one thought burning in his mind. He had to warn Jeff before it was too late. The searing pain in his back and chest told Billy-Joe that it was already too late for him.

It was a long way to the stables and his sight was

blurring. Something warm and sticky was dribbling down his chin. The road kept moving around all over the place. He fell on his face but pushed himself up and staggered on.

Then, out of nowhere, a big pair of arms grabbed him cradled him like a yearling. His face felt wet. He opened his eyes to see tears running down Jeff's face, they were falling on his as the big man held him.

He'd never been loved like this since his daddy died.

The voice broke through his thoughts. 'Who, son? Tell me who did it?'

Billy-Joe smiled softly, things were beginning to drift away from him. His lips moved but no sound came. He wanted desperately to warn his good friend.

Jeff leaned over placing his ear close to the boy's mouth. 'Tell me, son,' he pleaded.

Billy-Joe's lips moved again. 'He ... he's at the bank—'

The last whispered word turned into a sigh as the lad's body relaxed in death.

Slowly Jeff lowered the boy into the street. He drew and checked his guns.

Today a man was going to die, to pay for the carnage he had caused, for the money he had tried to steal, but most of all for Billy-Joe.

As if in a dream, but acutely aware of everything going on around him, Jeff paced slowly towards the bank at the end of the street.

One horse stood at the hitching rail at this early hour, the bank had only been open a short while.

The doors were flung open and a man emerged carrying a large carpet-bag. He saw Mason and recognition and incredulity flashed across his face then was gone in a second as he allowed the bag to fall to the floor, his hands dipping for the matched pistols.

Jeff was stunned into immobility. This man was dead; Billy-Joe had seen the blood on his saddle that night when McBride had brought the horse back without its rider!

The shock almost got him killed as a bullet ploughed between his inner arm and side, then instinct took over.

His guns seemed to flow into his hands, each bullet finding its mark as bullet after bullet punched into Sam Pinter, pushing him upright as he jerked spasmodically to every punishing shot.

Both guns clicked on empty before Jeff pushed the guns into his holsters. Then he picked up the carpet-bag and walked slowly back to that small limp form in the middle of the road....